Disney

Tim Burton's THE NIGHTMARE BEFORE CHRISTMAS

ALSO FROM JOE BOOKS

Disney Moana Movie Graphic Novel

Disney Pirates of the Caribbean: Dead Men Tell No Tales Movie Graphic Novel

Disney • Pixar Cars Movie Graphic Novel

Disney • Pixar Cars 3 Movie Graphic Novel

Disney Tangled: The Story of the Movie in Comics

Disney Snow White and the Seven Dwarfs: The Story of the Movie in Comics

Disney The Lion King: The Story of the Movie in Comics

Disney The Little Mermaid: The Story of the Movie in Comics

Disney Lilo & Stitch: The Story of the Movie in Comics

Disney The Princess and the Frog: The Story of the Movie in Comics

DISNEP

TIM BURTON'S
THE
NIGHTMARE
BEFORE
CHRISTMAS

JOE BOOKS

Published simultaneously in the United States and Canada by Joe Books Ltd,
489 College Street, Suite 203, Toronto, ON M6G 1A5.

www.joebooks.com

First Joe Books edition: July 2018

ISBN: 978-1-77275-808-5

Library and Archives Canada Cataloguing in Publication
information is available upon request.

Printed and bound in Canada
1 3 5 7 9 10 8 6 4 2

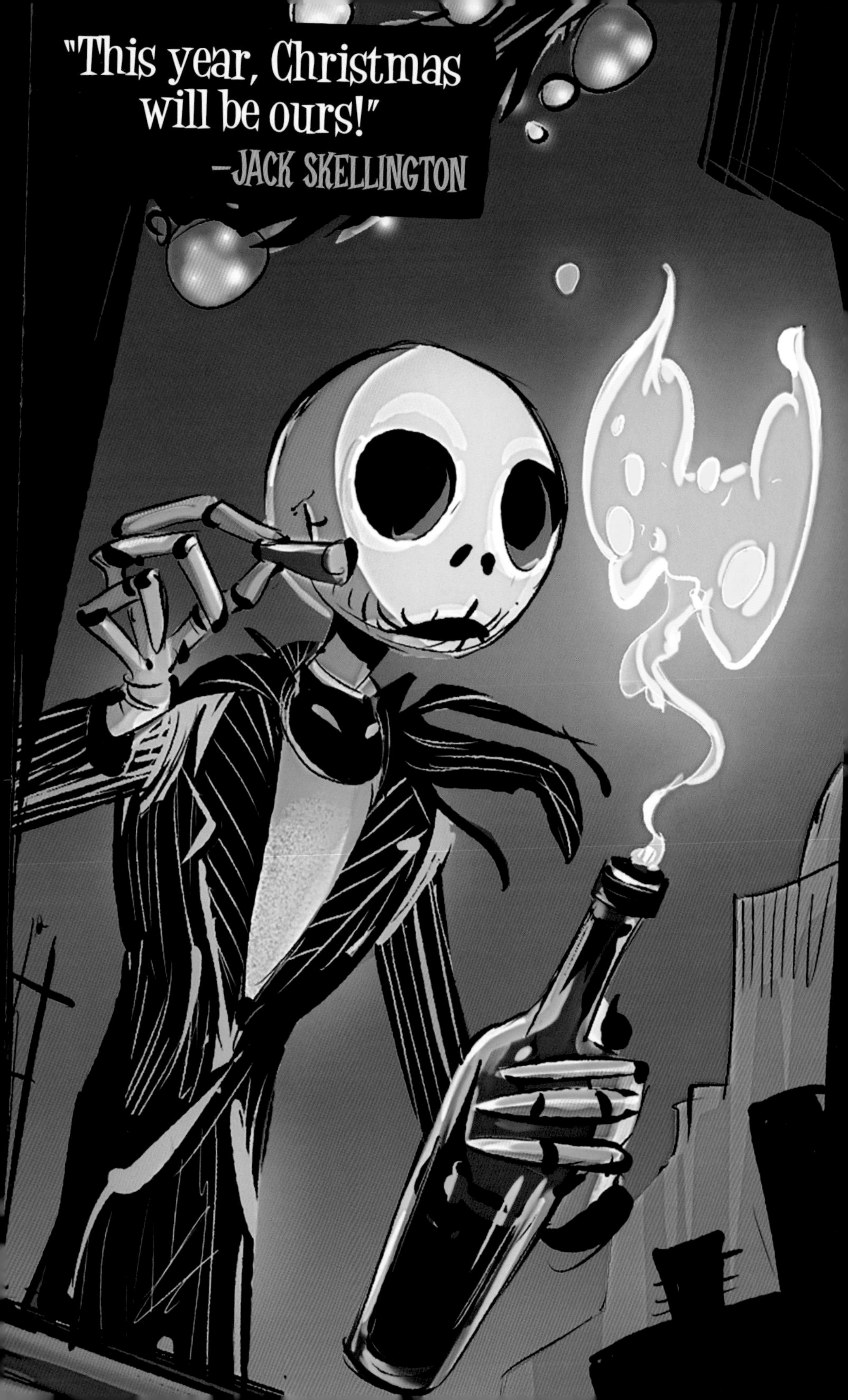
"This year, Christmas will be ours!"
–JACK SKELLINGTON

JACK SKELLINGTON

Jack Skellington, the tall and thin Pumpkin King of Halloween Town, is a terrifying skeleton who could chill the bravest men with a simple whisper. But despite his blood-curdling smile, Jack is gentle, kind, and patient at heart. And he wants more than just to frighten people. Lonely and melancholy, Jack is looking for something new, something other than the usual Halloween Night...

...RO

...ck's loyal and playful ghost ...og is never far from him. ...o usually spends most of the ... sleeping at home or at the ...etery, but he is always ready to ...w Jack for a walk or to play ... with Jack's ribs. Although ...ay not always understand his ...

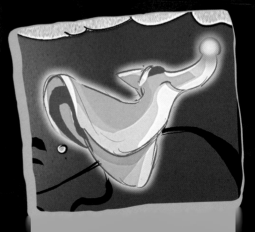

SALLY

Created by Dr. Finklestein, Sally is a rag doll made of different pieces stitched together and stuffed with autumn leaves. Each piece has a life of its own, and can detach and move independently, so Sally can always put herself back together again with a needle and thread. Resourceful and brave, Sally is Jack's truest friend. Like him, she yearns for something else from life.

SANTA CLAUS

Jolly and caring, Santa Claus is the ruler of Christmas Town and, like Jack, works all year to prepare for one night. Everything about Santa fascinates the Pumpkin King, especially his name—which Jack actually mishears as Sandy Claws! Despite his big build, Santa Claus can easily get through narrow spaces like the chimneys of most houses.

THE MAYOR

*V*erbose, insecure, and badly equipped to handle emergencies, the Mayor of Halloween Town cannot make any decision alone—not even the easiest ones, like planning the next Halloween. He is literally two faced: when he is happy, the Mayor shows a smiley face, and when he is worried, his head turns and displays a rather concerned expression.

DR. FINKLESTEIN

*T*he Evil Scientist of Halloween Town and a well-known genius, Dr. Finklestein is the creator of Sally, and considers her his best and most precious work. It is for this reason that Finklestein holds her prisoner—unsuccessfully, most of the time—in his house. Finklestein's head is a metal plate that he can open to rub his brain when he needs to focus on something.

OOGIE BOOGIE

*H*is lair is a strange and spooky gambling den, lit by ultraviolet lights and filled with torture devices. Mr. Oogie Boogie's body is made of countless creepy bugs contained in a burlap sack, and his soul is just as sinister. Oogie Boogie is the ultimate nightmare—the meanest, most evil citizen of Halloween Town, and its only true villain. He only fears Jack Skellington. Oogie Boogie loves gambling, but he has no skill for it and cheats most of the time!

LOCK, SHOCK & BARREL

*T*he best trick-or-treaters in Halloween Town, these three mischievous little demons travel around in a walking bathtub and live in a tree house outside the city, just above Mr. Oogie Boogie's lair. They usually work for Oogie Boogie, but occasionally they'll accept a job from Jack Skellington. They all wear masks: Lock wears a devil mask, Shock, a witch mask, and Barrel, a ghoul mask. But strangely enough, their faces look exactly like their masks!

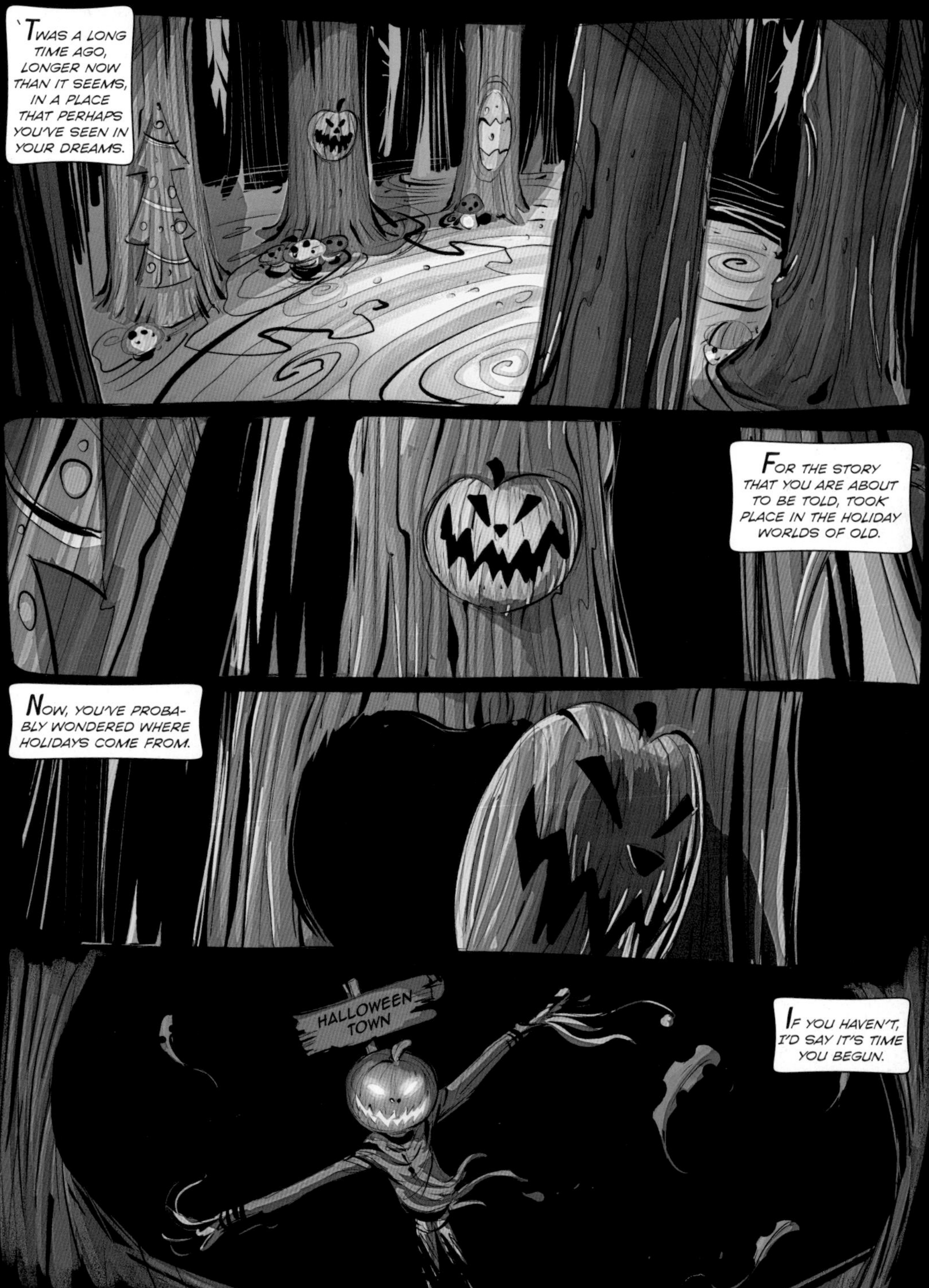
`TWAS A LONG TIME AGO, LONGER NOW THAN IT SEEMS, IN A PLACE THAT PERHAPS YOU'VE SEEN IN YOUR DREAMS.
FOR THE STORY THAT YOU ARE ABOUT TO BE TOLD, TOOK PLACE IN THE HOLIDAY WORLDS OF OLD.
NOW, YOU'VE PROBABLY WONDERED WHERE HOLIDAYS COME FROM.
HALLOWEEN TOWN
IF YOU HAVEN'T, I'D SAY IT'S TIME YOU BEGUN.

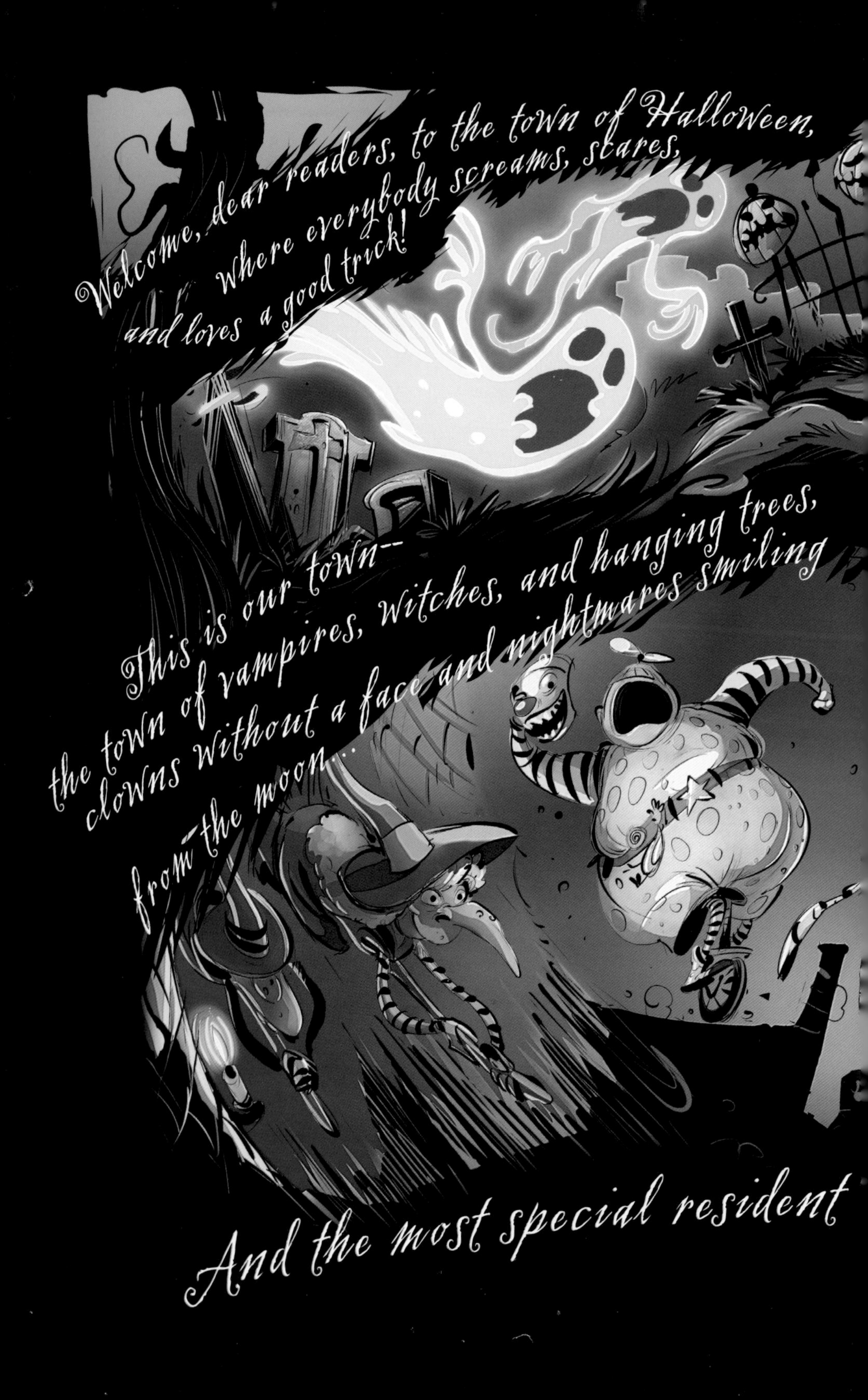

Welcome, dear readers, to the town of Halloween, where everybody screams, scares, and loves a good trick!

This is our town—the town of vampires, witches, and hanging trees, clowns without a face and nightmares smiling from the moon...

And the most special resident

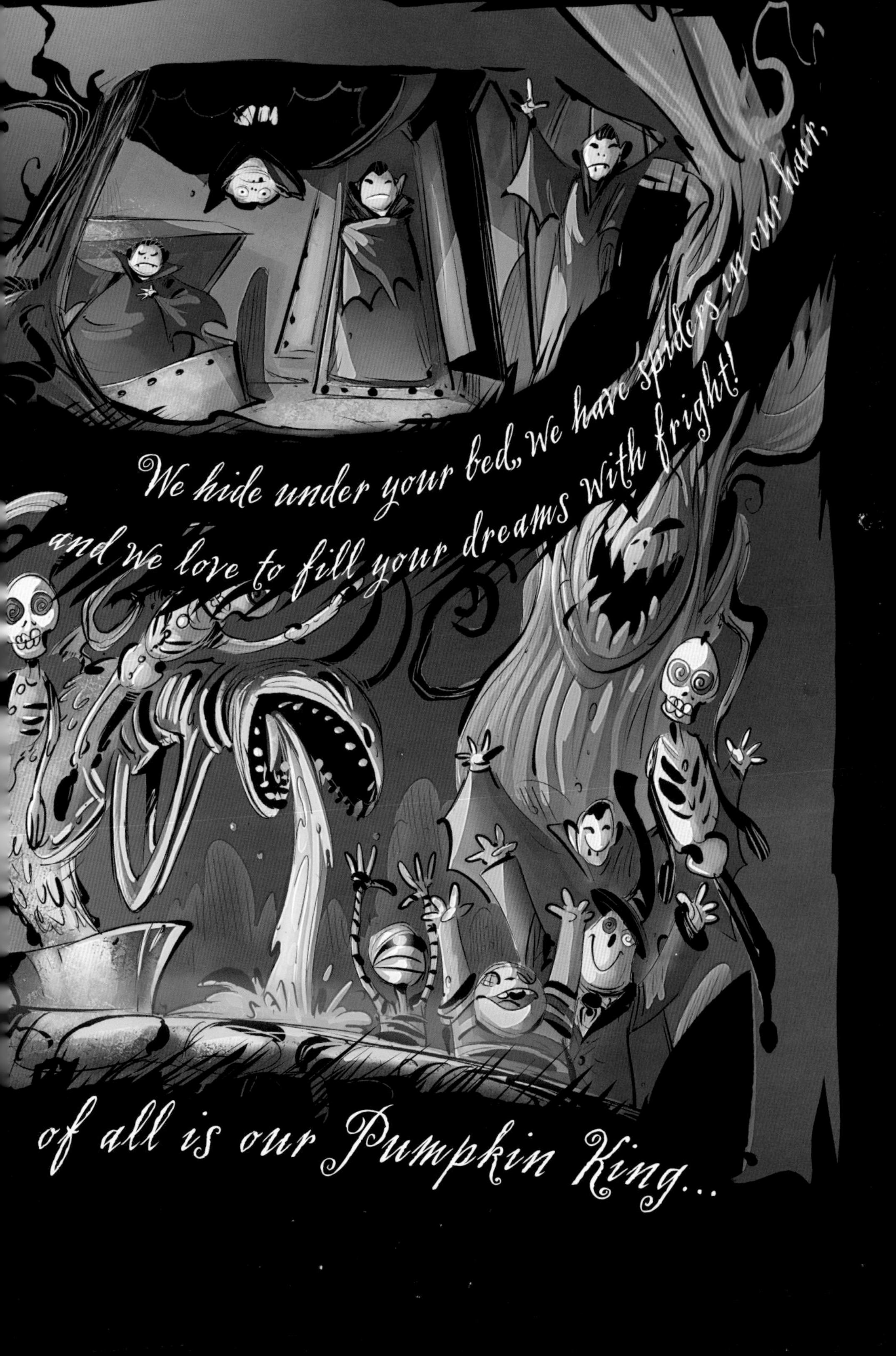
We hide under your bed, we have spiders in our hair,
and we love to fill your dreams with fright!
of all is our Pumpkin King...

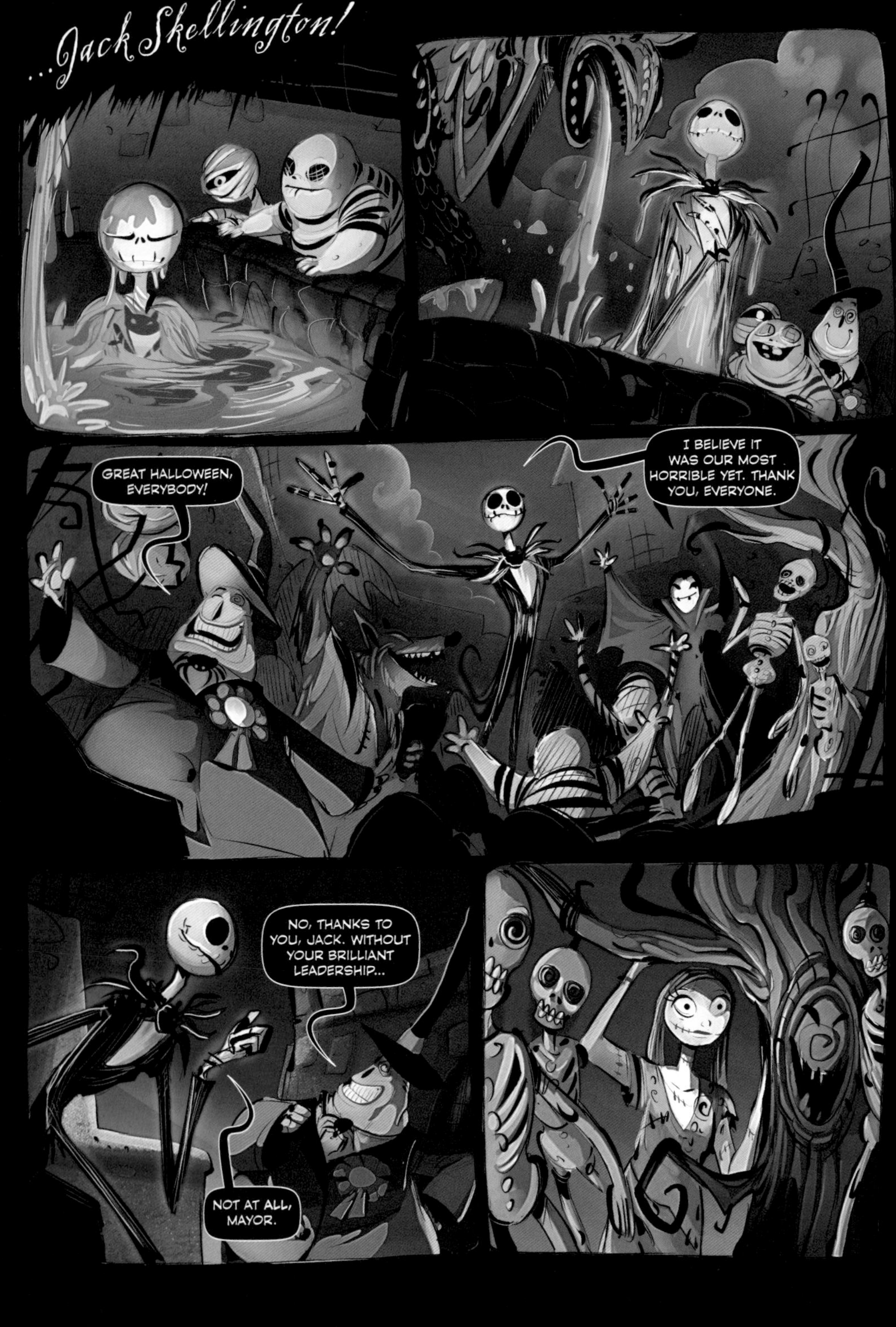

...Jack Skellington!
GREAT HALLOWEEN, EVERYBODY!
I BELIEVE IT WAS OUR MOST HORRIBLE YET. THANK YOU, EVERYONE.
NO, THANKS TO YOU, JACK. WITHOUT YOUR BRILLIANT LEADERSHIP...
NOT AT ALL, MAYOR.

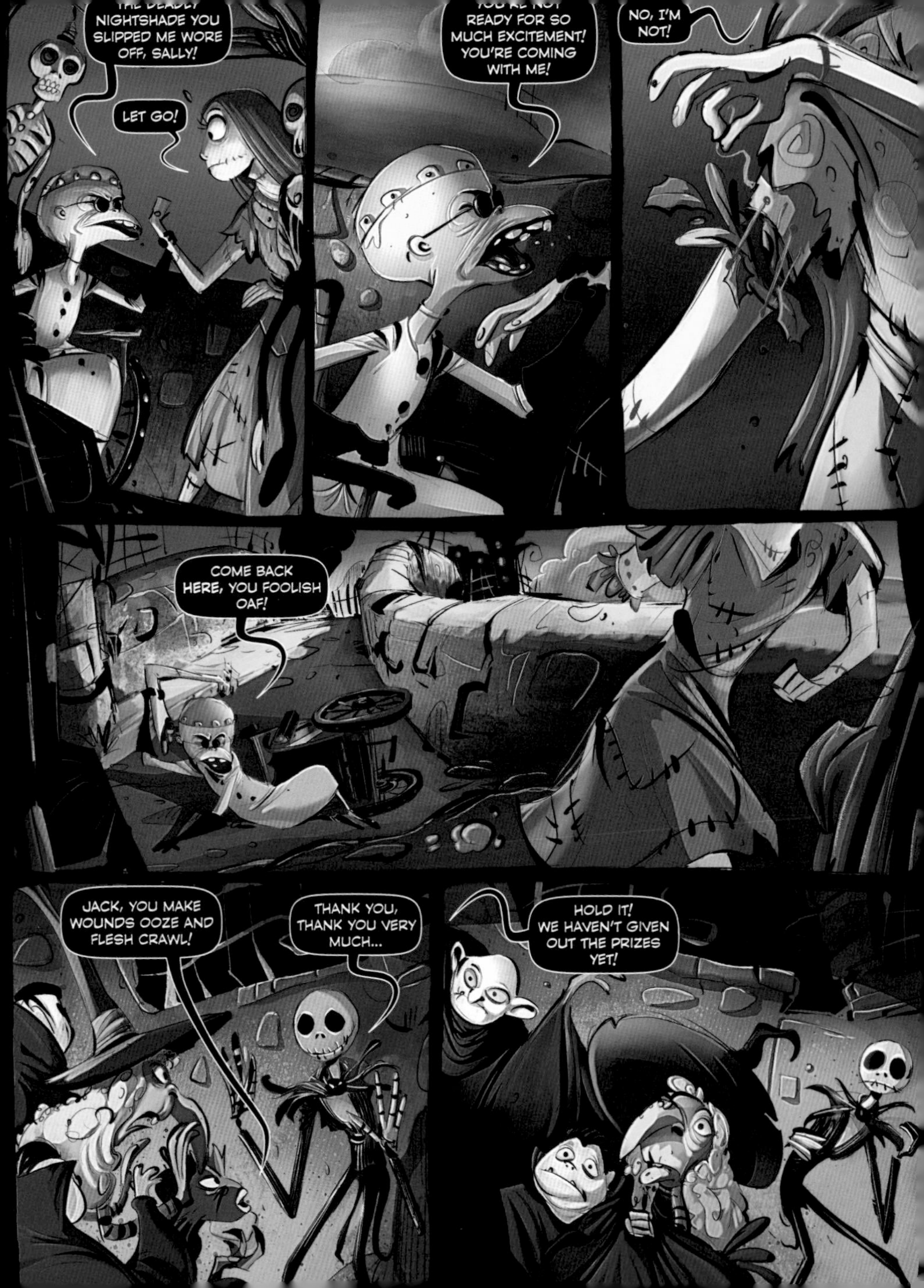
NIGHTSHADE YOU SLIPPED ME WORE OFF, SALLY!
LET GO!
READY FOR SO MUCH EXCITEMENT! YOU'RE COMING WITH ME!
NO, I'M NOT!
COME BACK HERE, YOU FOOLISH OAF!
JACK, YOU MAKE WOUNDS OOZE AND FLESH CRAWL!
THANK YOU, THANK YOU VERY MUCH...
HOLD IT! WE HAVEN'T GIVEN OUT THE PRIZES YET!

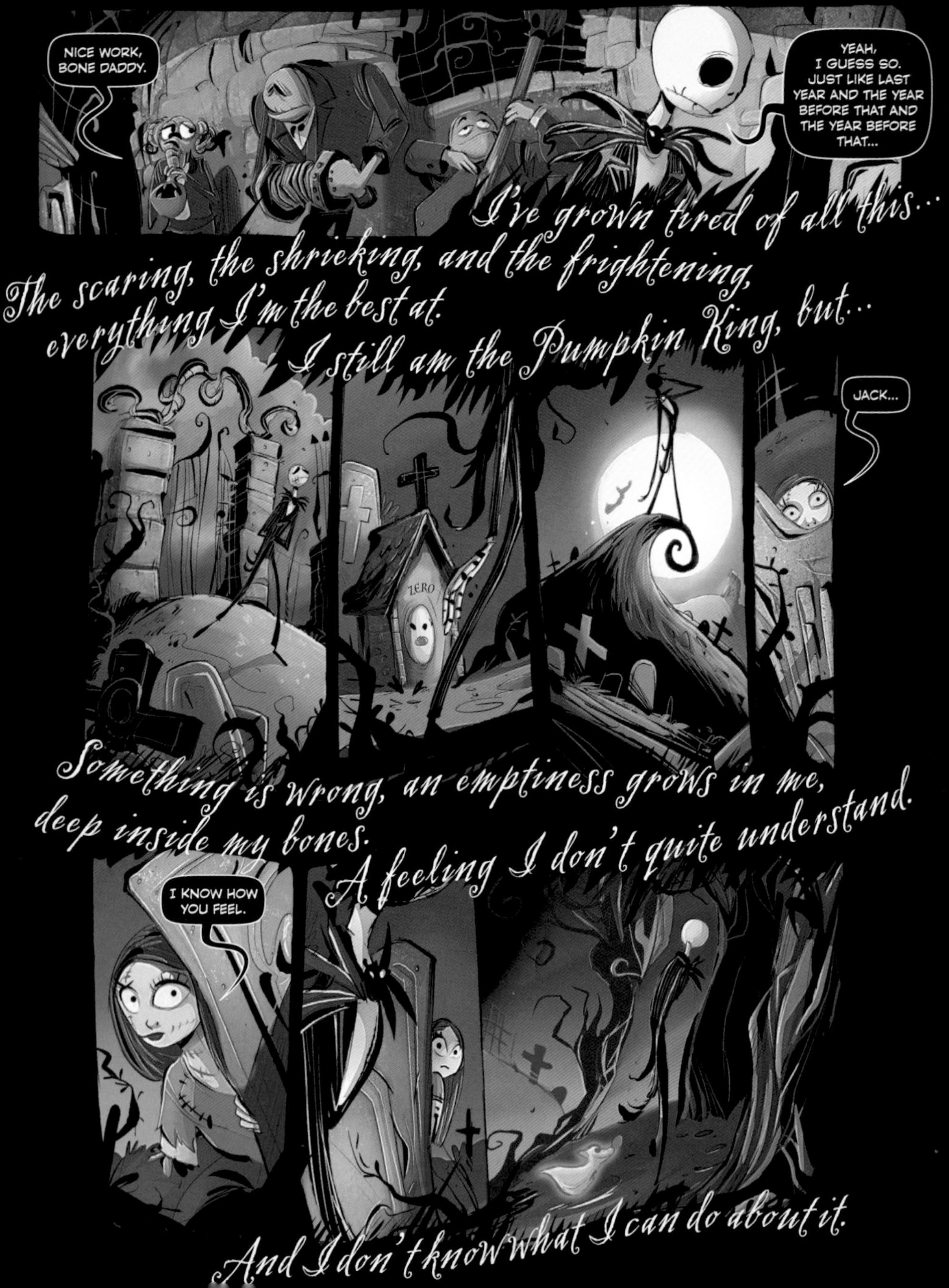
NICE WORK, BONE DADDY.
YEAH, I GUESS SO. JUST LIKE LAST YEAR AND THE YEAR BEFORE THAT AND THE YEAR BEFORE THAT...
I've grown tired of all this...
The scaring, the shrieking, and the frightening,
everything I'm the best at.
I still am the Pumpkin King, but...
JACK...
Something is wrong, an emptiness grows in me,
deep inside my bones.
A feeling I don't quite understand.
I KNOW HOW YOU FEEL.
And I don't know what I can do about it.

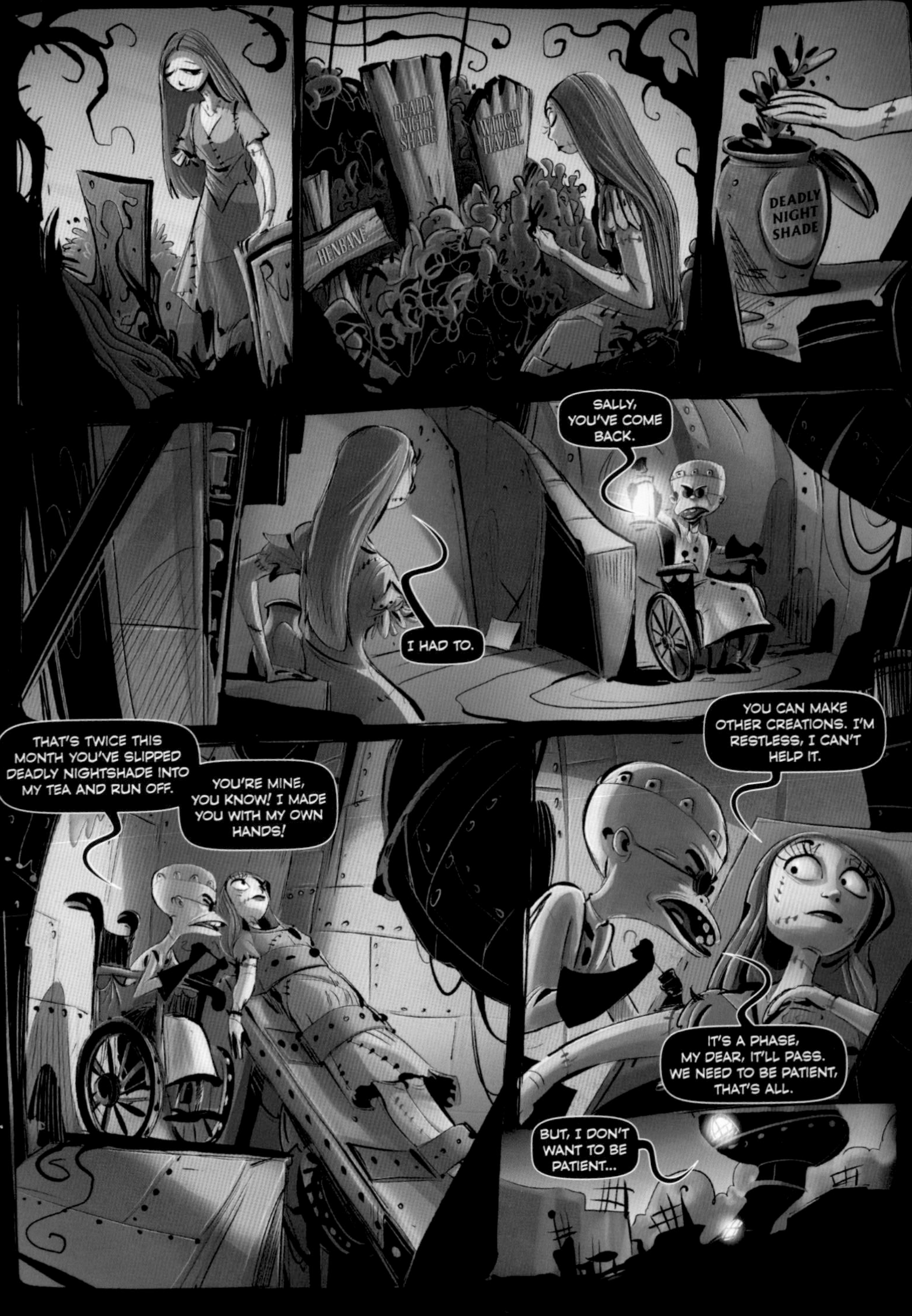
DEADLY NIGHT SHADE
WITCH HAZEL
HENBANE
DEADLY NIGHT SHADE
SALLY, YOU'VE COME BACK.
I HAD TO.
THAT'S TWICE THIS MONTH YOU'VE SLIPPED DEADLY NIGHTSHADE INTO MY TEA AND RUN OFF.
YOU'RE MINE, YOU KNOW! I MADE YOU WITH MY OWN HANDS!
YOU CAN MAKE OTHER CREATIONS. I'M RESTLESS, I CAN'T HELP IT.
IT'S A PHASE, MY DEAR, IT'LL PASS. WE NEED TO BE PATIENT, THAT'S ALL.
BUT, I DON'T WANT TO BE PATIENT...

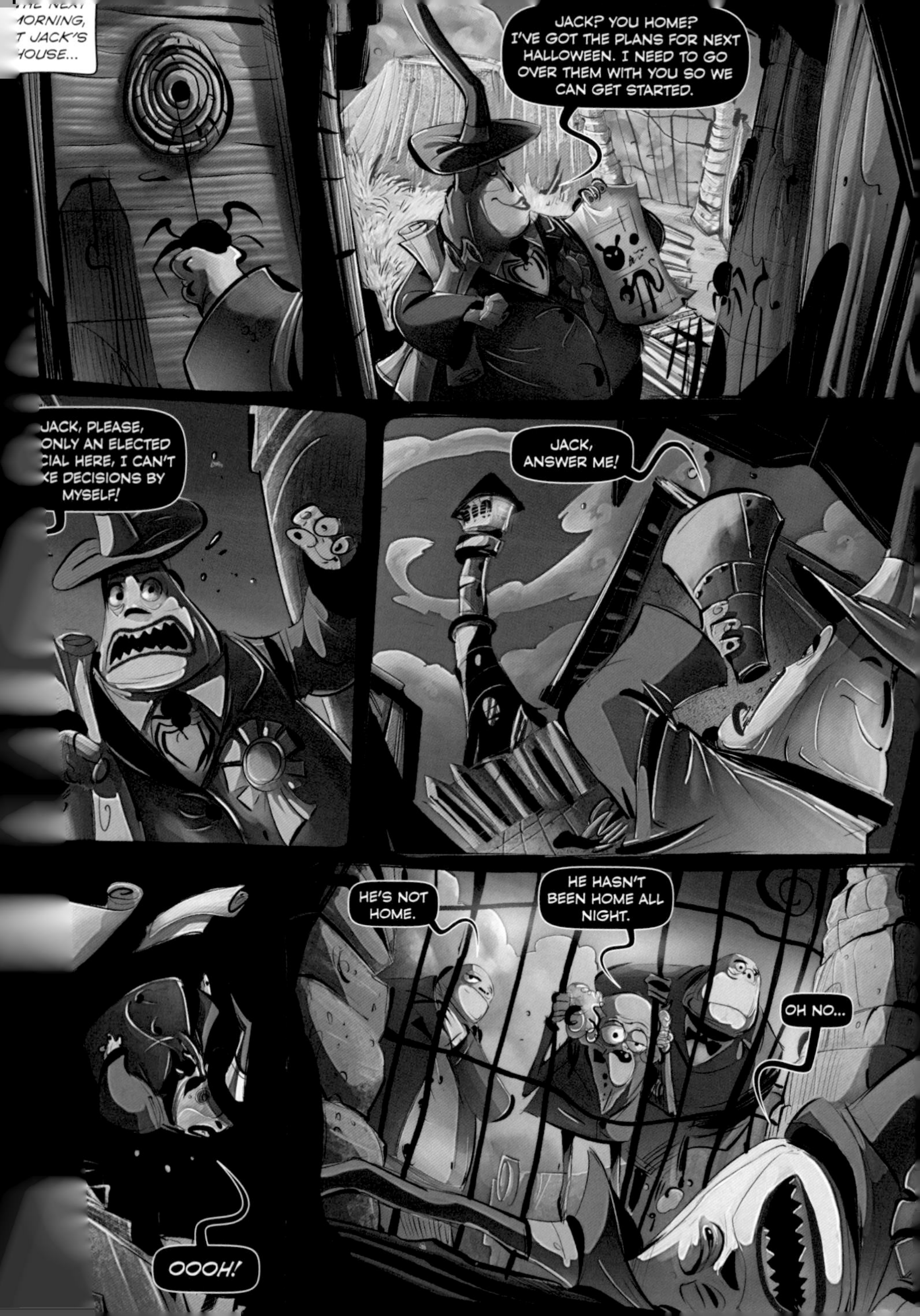
ORNING, T JACK'S IOUSE...
JACK? YOU HOME? I'VE GOT THE PLANS FOR NEXT HALLOWEEN. I NEED TO GO OVER THEM WITH YOU SO WE CAN GET STARTED.
JACK, PLEASE, ONLY AN ELECTED CIAL HERE, I CAN'T KE DECISIONS BY MYSELF!
JACK, ANSWER ME!
HE'S NOT HOME.
HE HASN'T BEEN HOME ALL NIGHT.
OH NO...
OOOH!

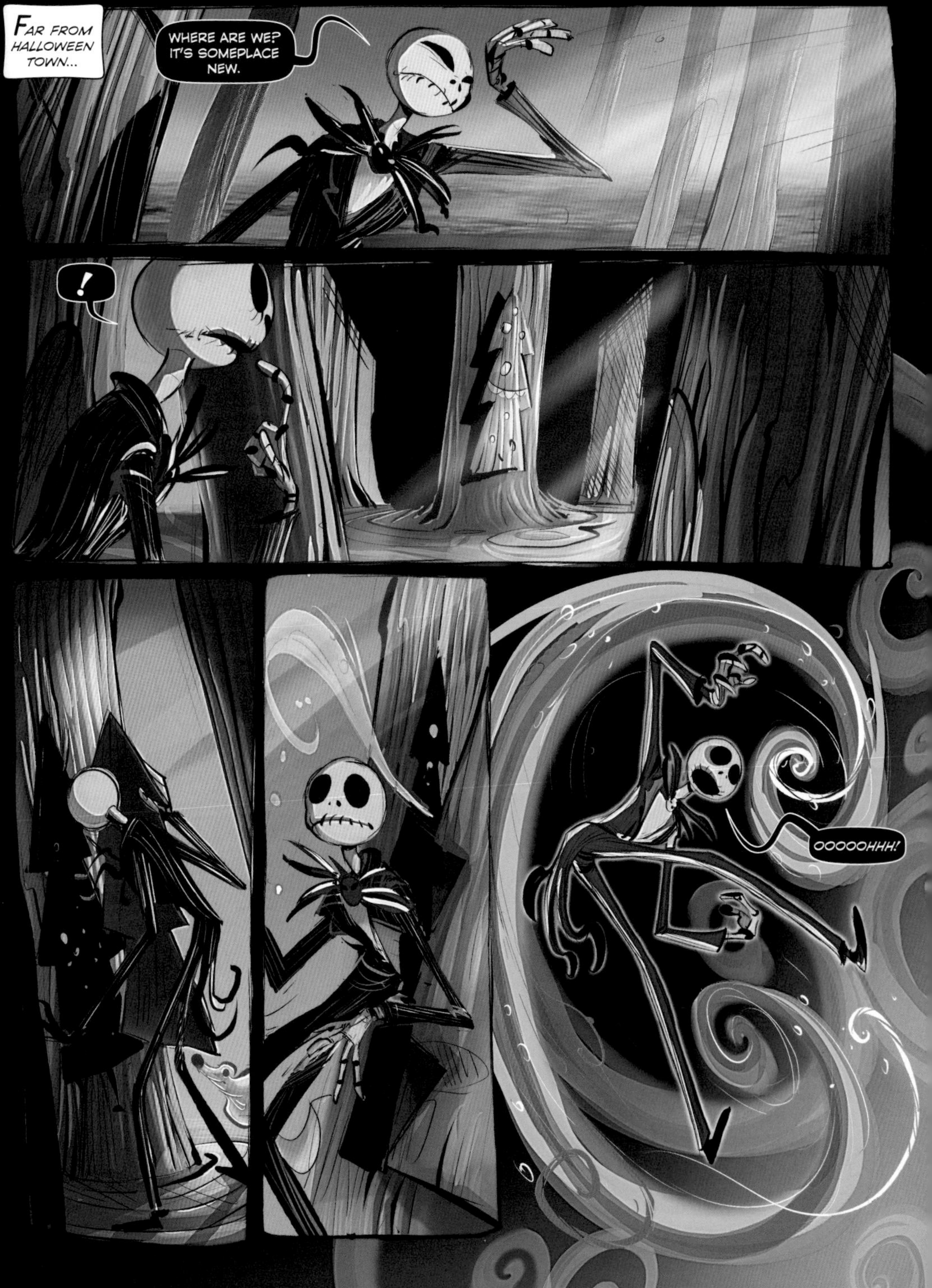
FAR FROM HALLOWEEN TOWN...
WHERE ARE WE? IT'S SOMEPLACE NEW.
!
OOOOOHHH!

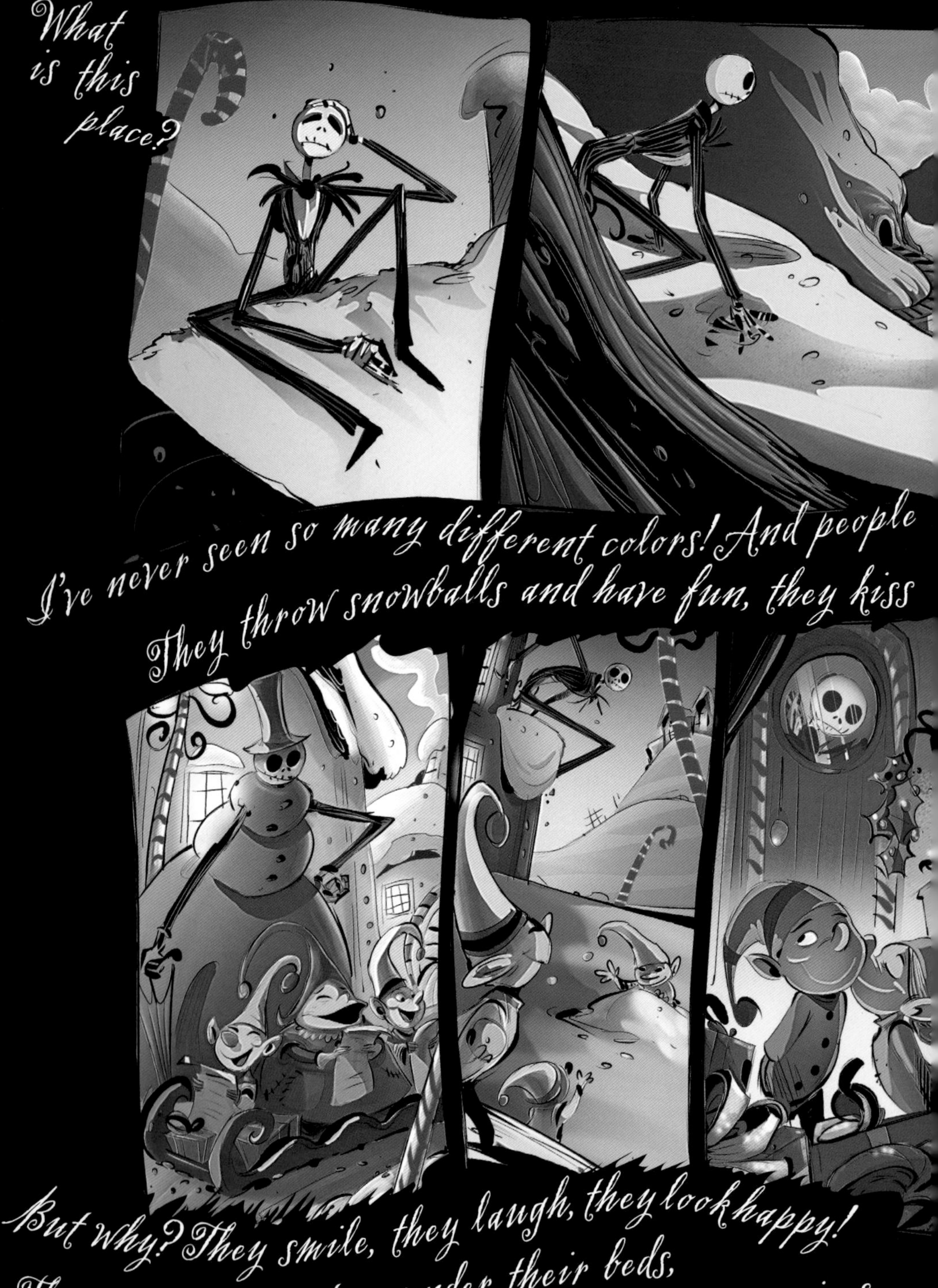
What is this place?
I've never seen so many different colors! And people
They throw snowballs and have fun, they kiss
But why? They smile, they laugh, they look happy!
There are no monsters under their beds,
no witches, no vampires...

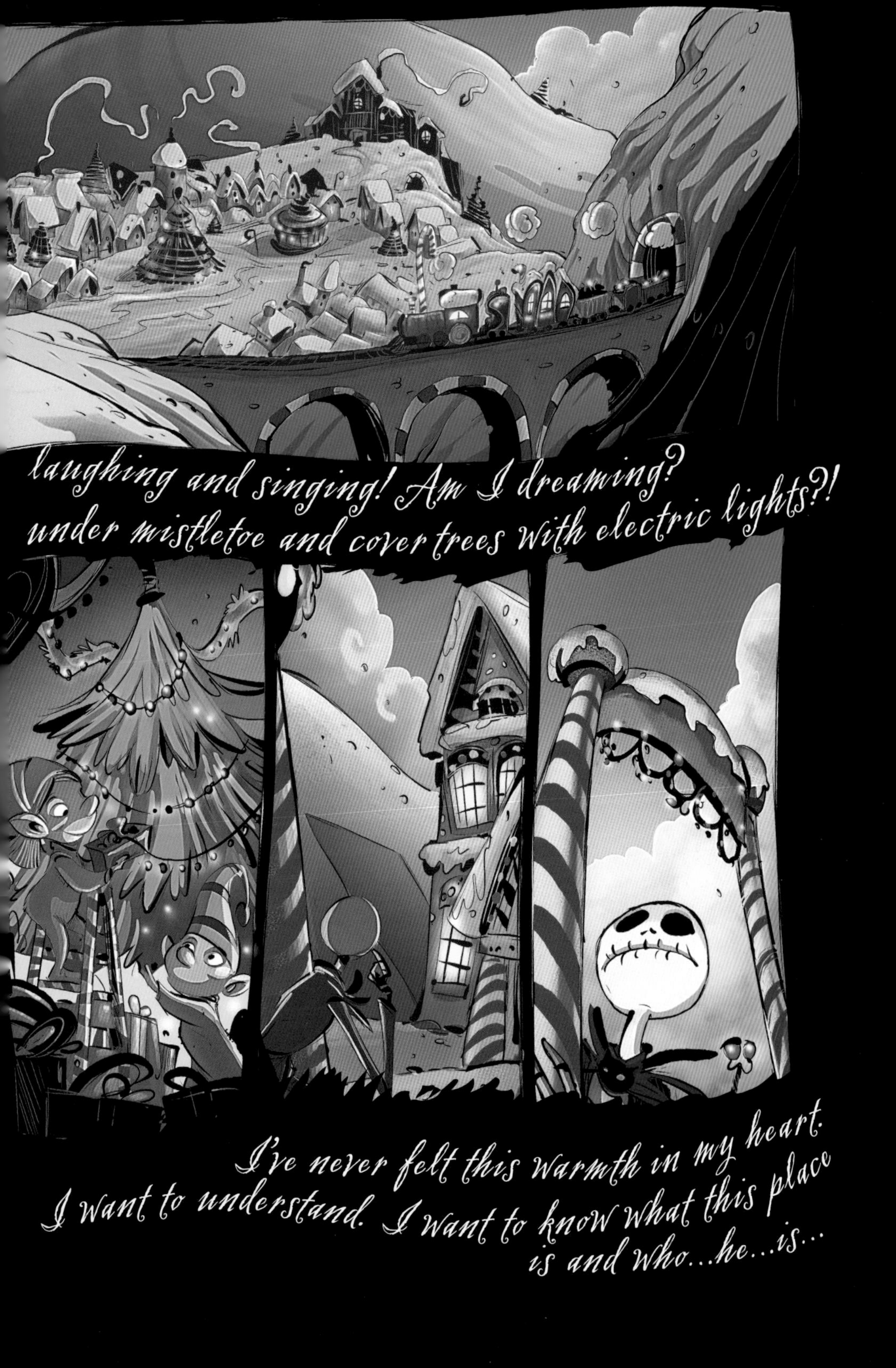
laughing and singing! Am I dreaming?
under mistletoe and cover trees with electric lights?!
I've never felt this warmth in my heart.
I want to understand. I want to know what this place is and who...he...is...

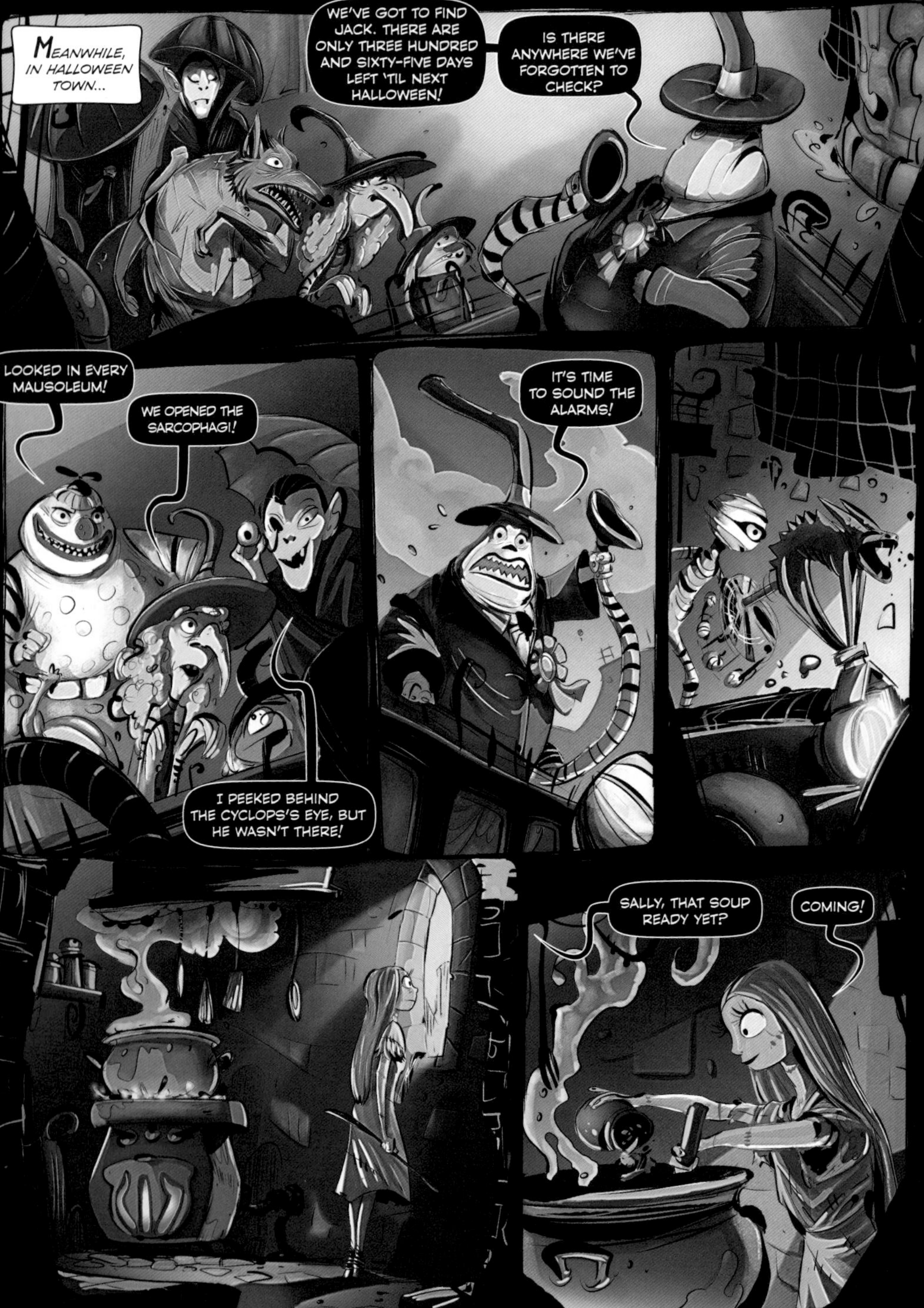
MEANWHILE, IN HALLOWEEN TOWN...
WE'VE GOT TO FIND JACK. THERE ARE ONLY THREE HUNDRED AND SIXTY-FIVE DAYS LEFT 'TIL NEXT HALLOWEEN!
IS THERE ANYWHERE WE'VE FORGOTTEN TO CHECK?
I LOOKED IN EVERY MAUSOLEUM!
WE OPENED THE SARCOPHAGI!
I PEEKED BEHIND THE CYCLOPS'S EYE, BUT HE WASN'T THERE!
IT'S TIME TO SOUND THE ALARMS!
SALLY, THAT SOUP READY YET?
COMING!

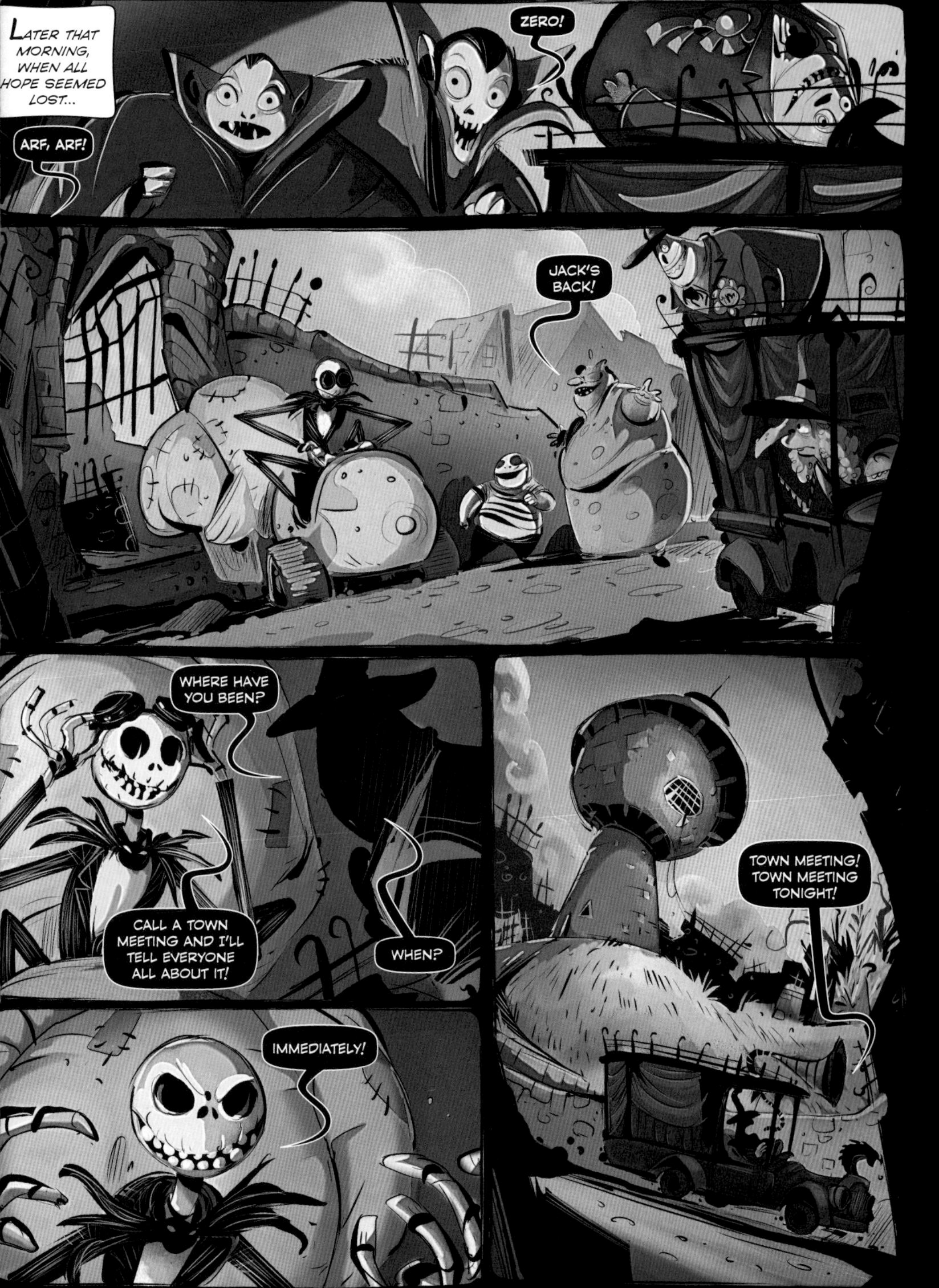
LATER THAT MORNING, WHEN ALL HOPE SEEMED LOST...
ARF, ARF!
ZERO!
JACK'S BACK!
WHERE HAVE YOU BEEN?
CALL A TOWN MEETING AND I'LL TELL EVERYONE ALL ABOUT IT!
WHEN?
IMMEDIATELY!
TOWN MEETING! TOWN MEETING TONIGHT!

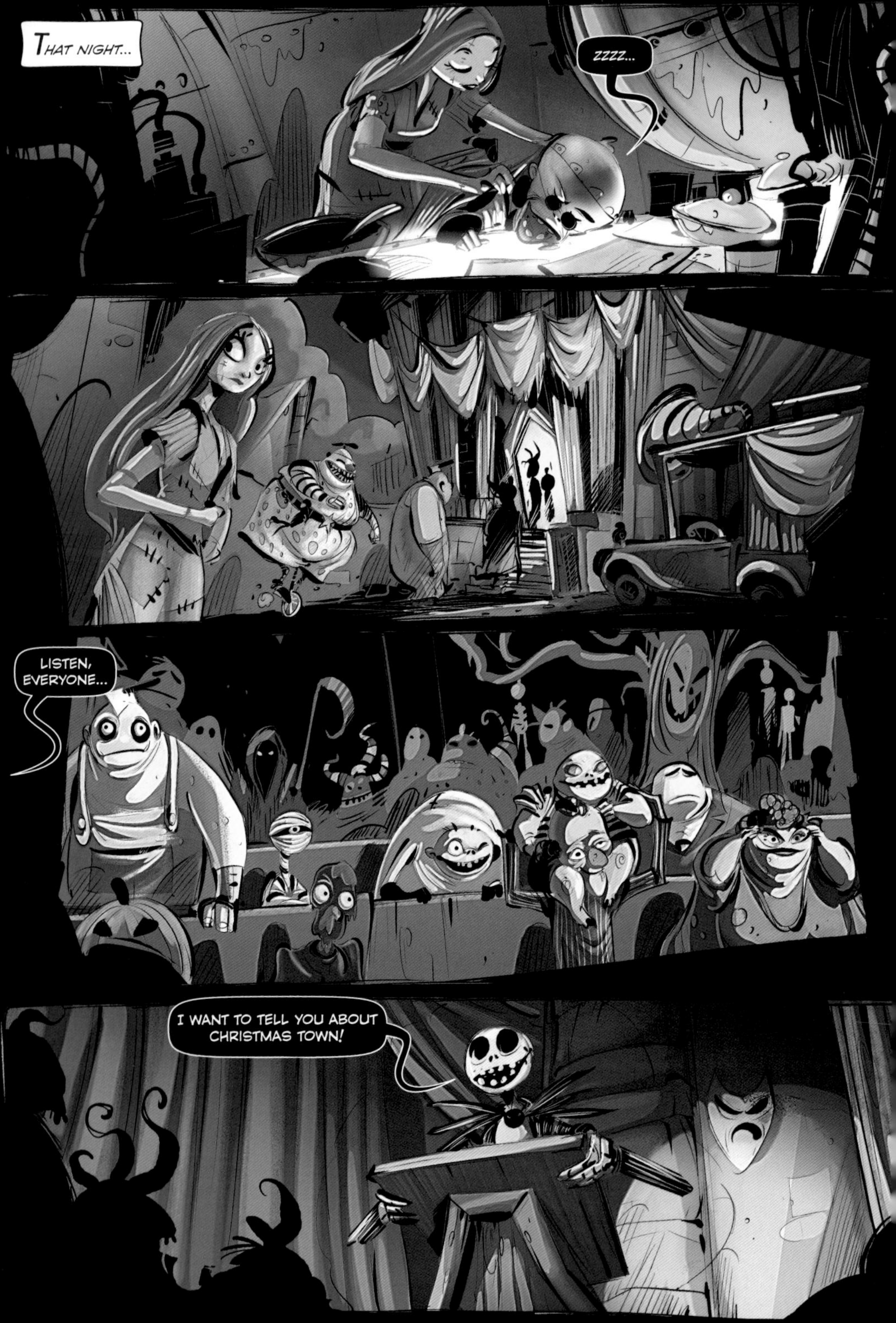
THAT NIGHT...
ZZZZ...
LISTEN, EVERYONE...
I WANT TO TELL YOU ABOUT CHRISTMAS TOWN!

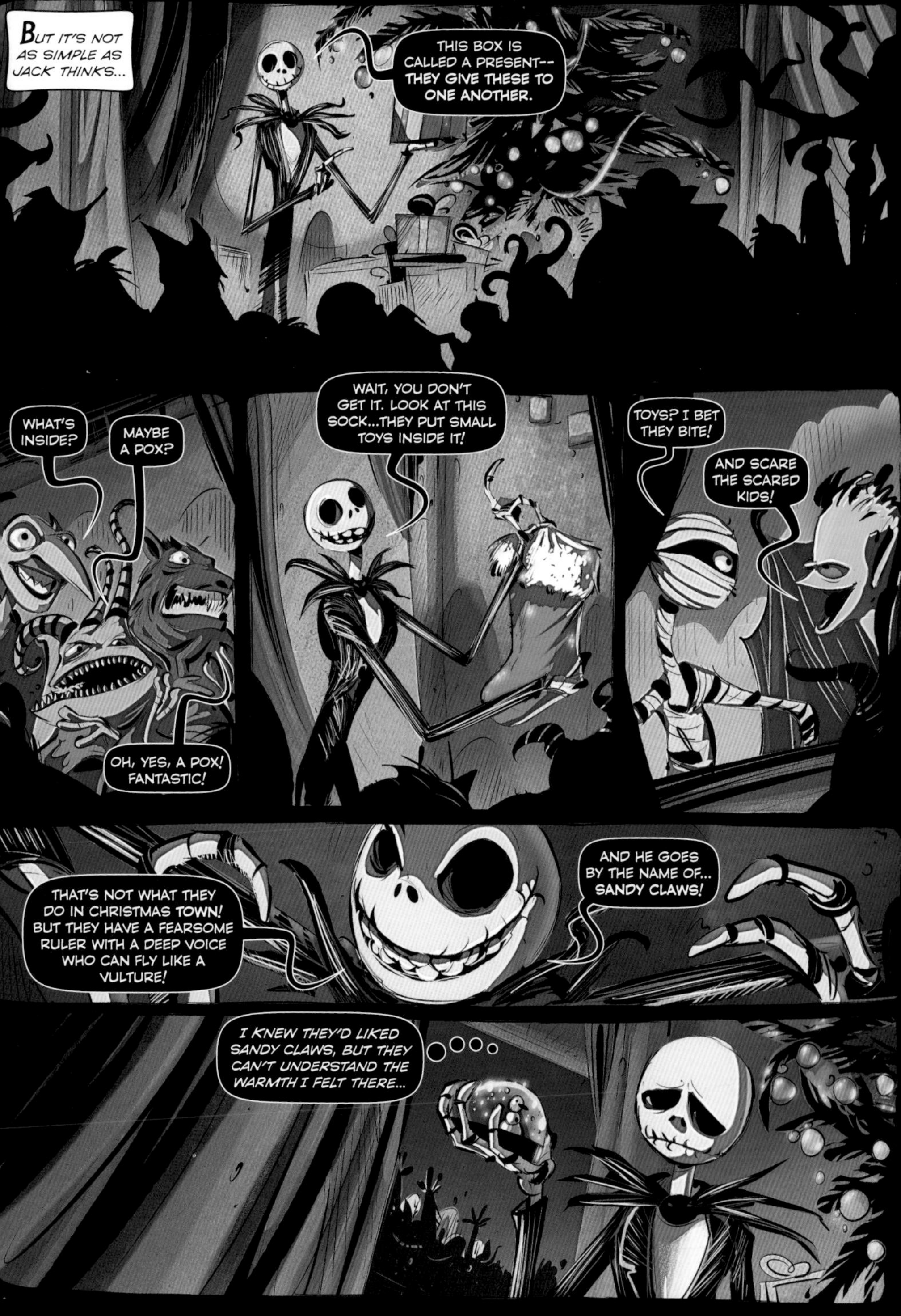
BUT IT'S NOT AS SIMPLE AS JACK THINKS...
THIS BOX IS CALLED A PRESENT-- THEY GIVE THESE TO ONE ANOTHER.
WHAT'S INSIDE?
MAYBE A POX?
OH, YES, A POX! FANTASTIC!
WAIT, YOU DON'T GET IT. LOOK AT THIS SOCK...THEY PUT SMALL TOYS INSIDE IT!
TOYS? I BET THEY BITE!
AND SCARE THE SCARED KIDS!
THAT'S NOT WHAT THEY DO IN CHRISTMAS TOWN! BUT THEY HAVE A FEARSOME RULER WITH A DEEP VOICE WHO CAN FLY LIKE A VULTURE!
AND HE GOES BY THE NAME OF... SANDY CLAWS!
I KNEW THEY'D LIKED SANDY CLAWS, BUT THEY CAN'T UNDERSTAND THE WARMTH I FELT THERE...

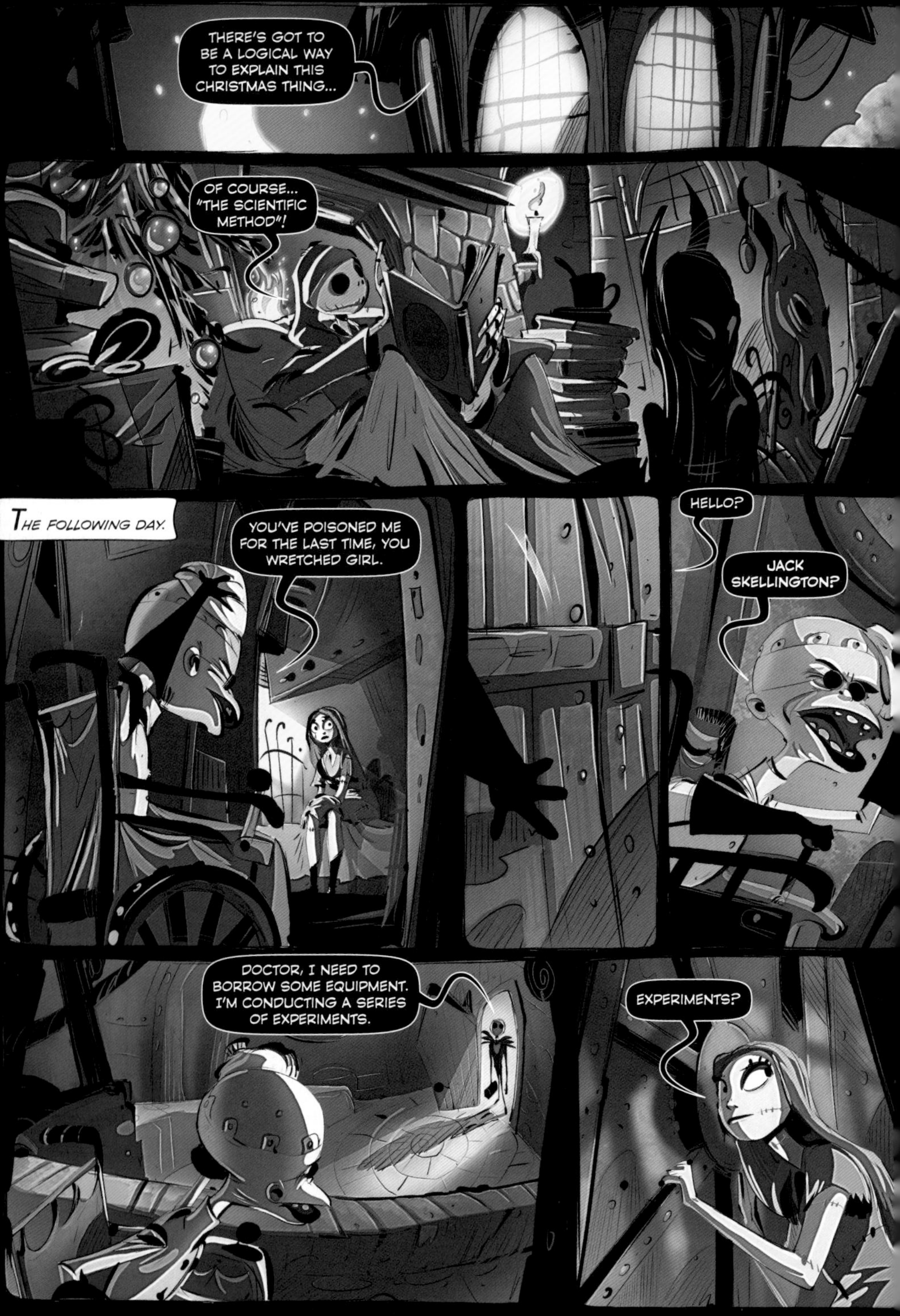

THERE'S GOT TO BE A LOGICAL WAY TO EXPLAIN THIS CHRISTMAS THING...
OF COURSE... "THE SCIENTIFIC METHOD"!
THE FOLLOWING DAY.
YOU'VE POISONED ME FOR THE LAST TIME, YOU WRETCHED GIRL.
HELLO?
JACK SKELLINGTON?
DOCTOR, I NEED TO BORROW SOME EQUIPMENT. I'M CONDUCTING A SERIES OF EXPERIMENTS.
EXPERIMENTS?

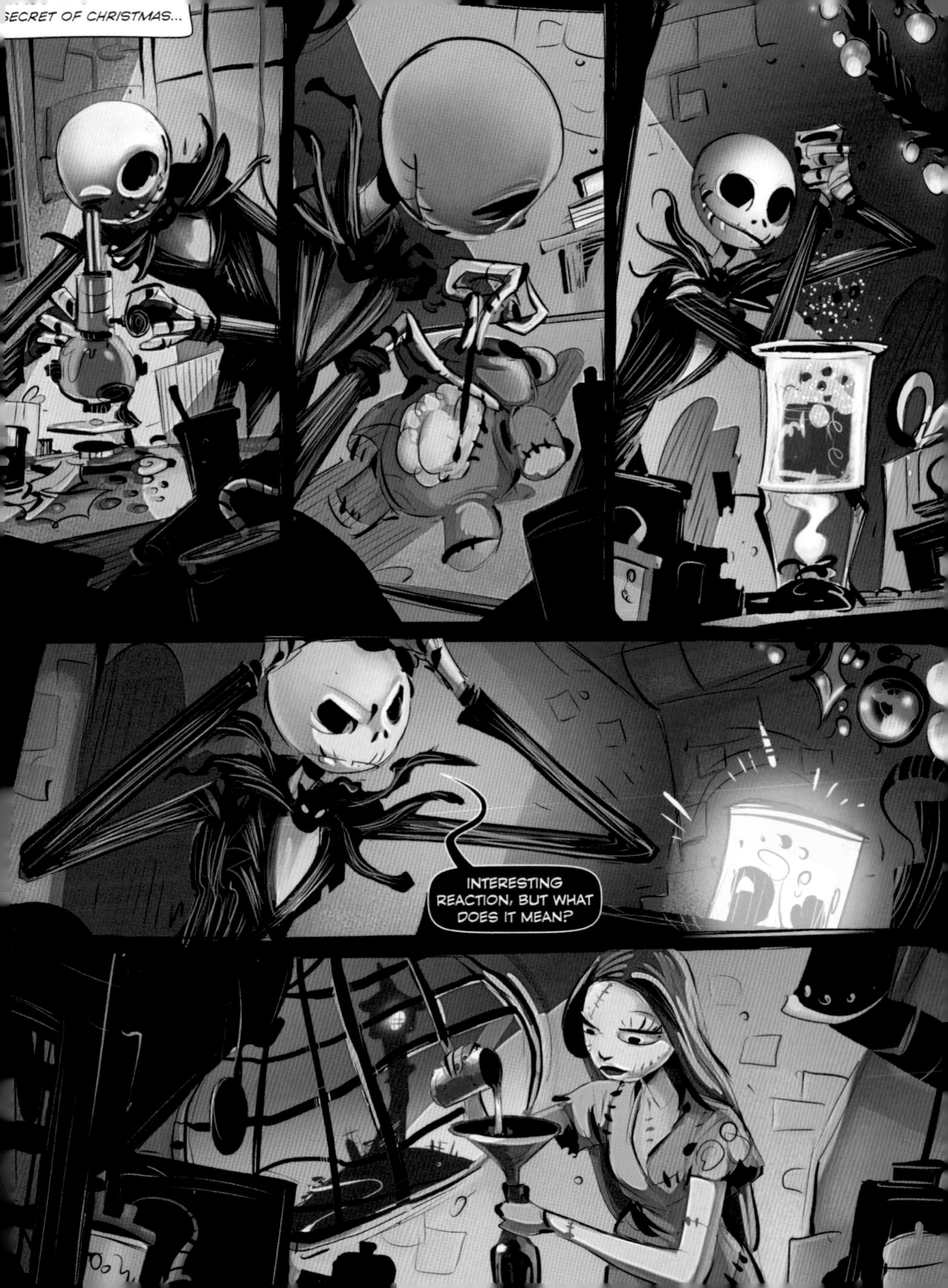
SECRET OF CHRISTMAS...
INTERESTING REACTION, BUT WHAT DOES IT MEAN?

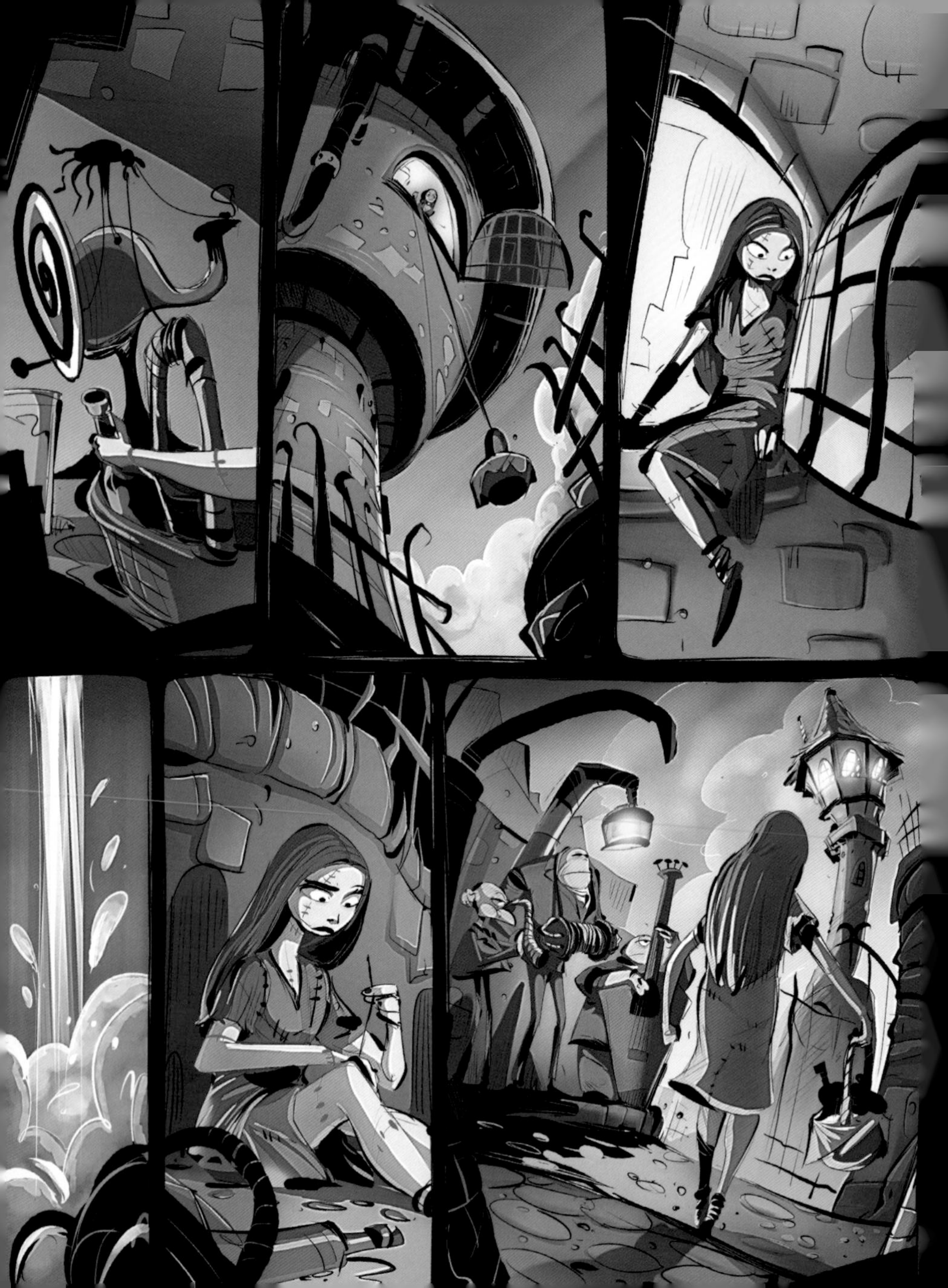

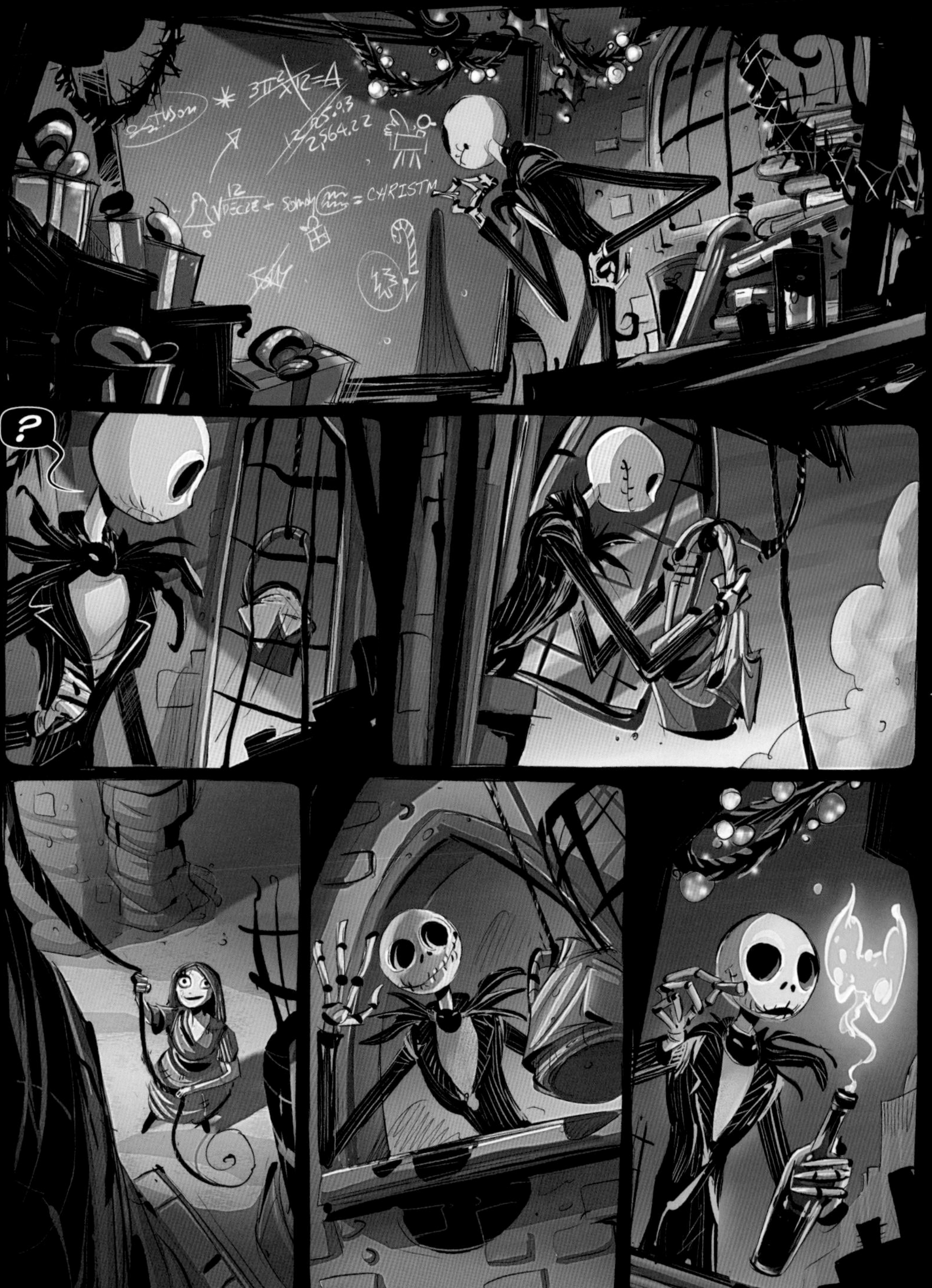
CHRISTM
?

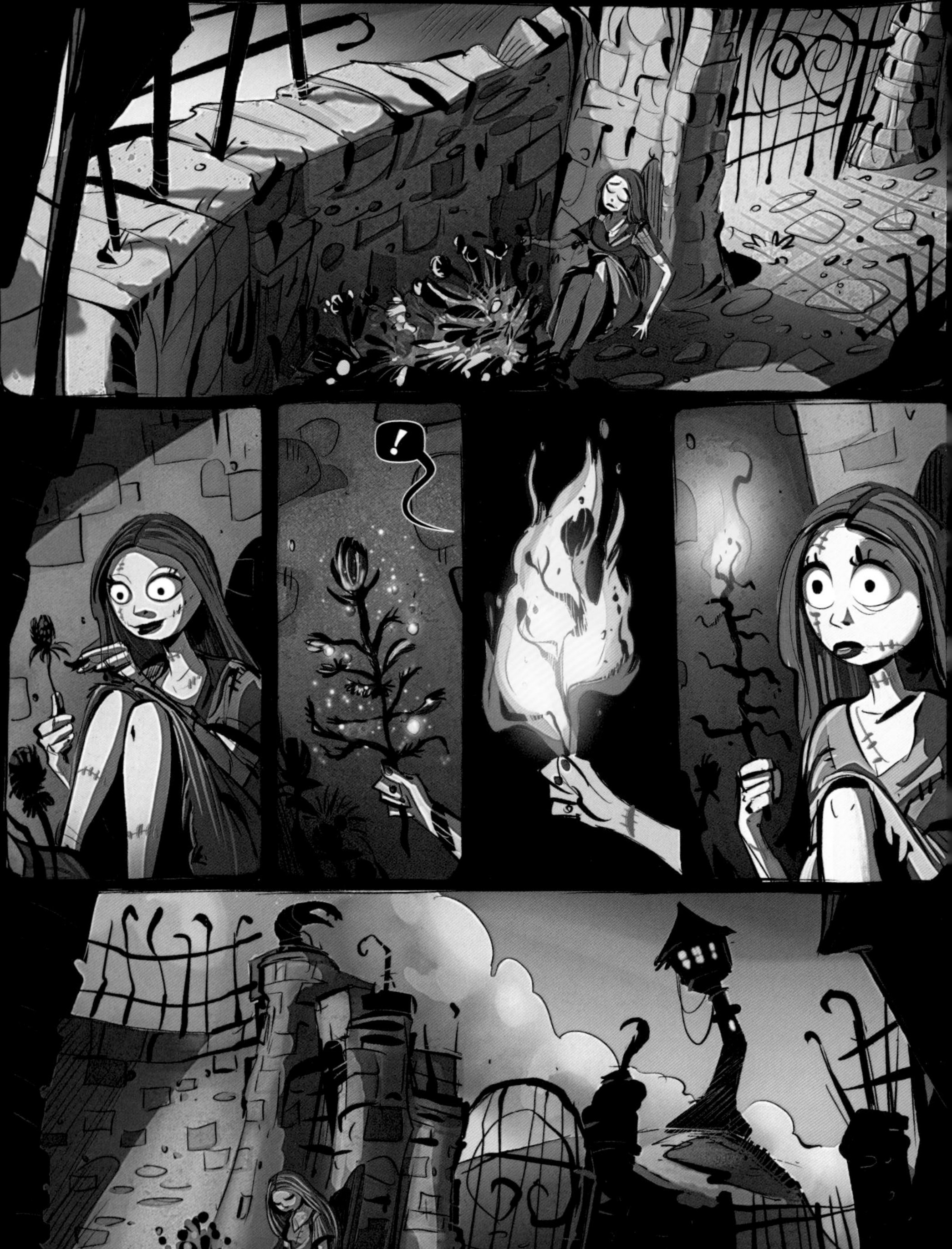
!

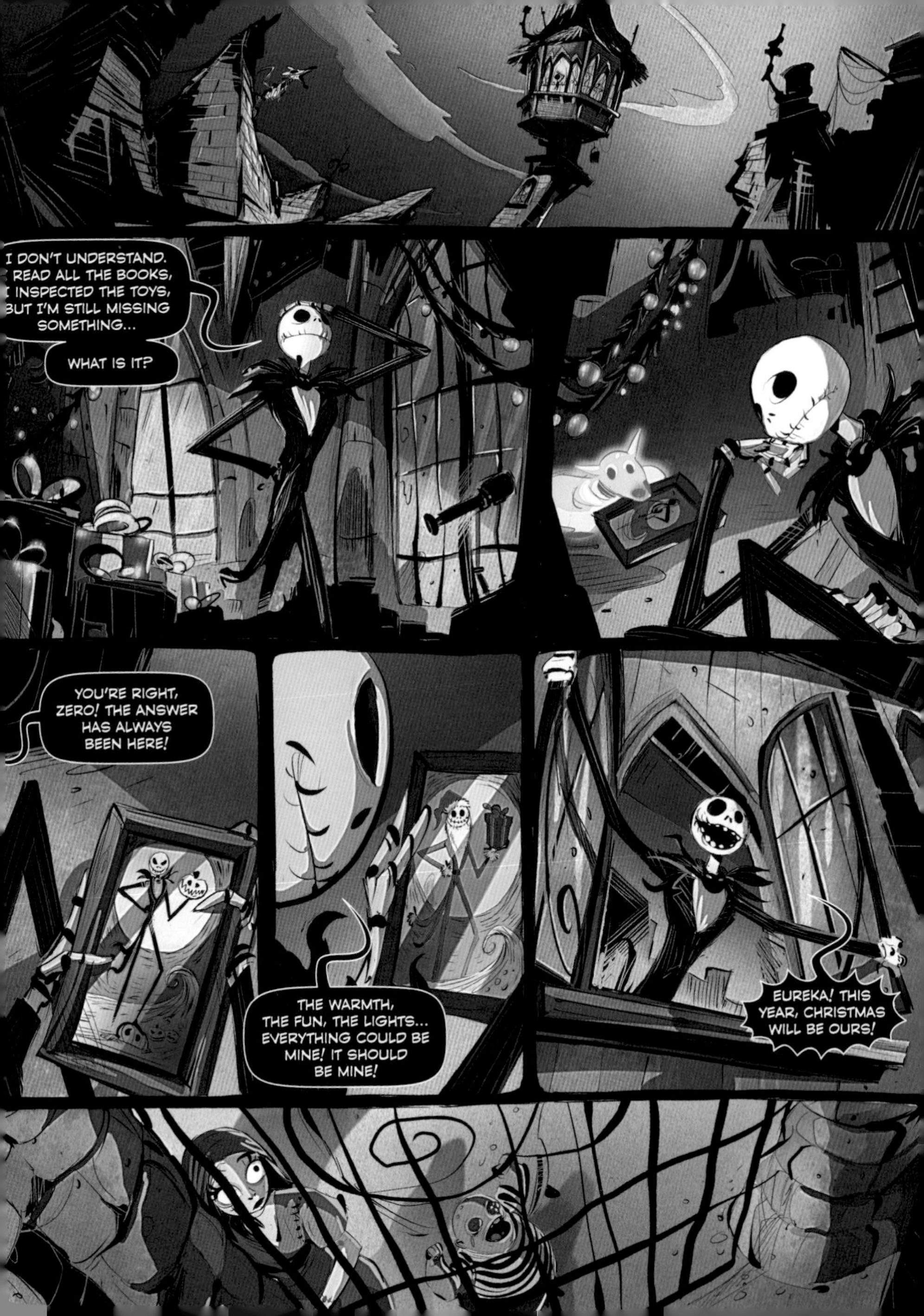
I DON'T UNDERSTAND. READ ALL THE BOOKS, I INSPECTED THE TOYS, BUT I'M STILL MISSING SOMETHING...
WHAT IS IT?
YOU'RE RIGHT, ZERO! THE ANSWER HAS ALWAYS BEEN HERE!
THE WARMTH, THE FUN, THE LIGHTS... EVERYTHING COULD BE MINE! IT SHOULD BE MINE!
EUREKA! THIS YEAR, CHRISTMAS WILL BE OURS!

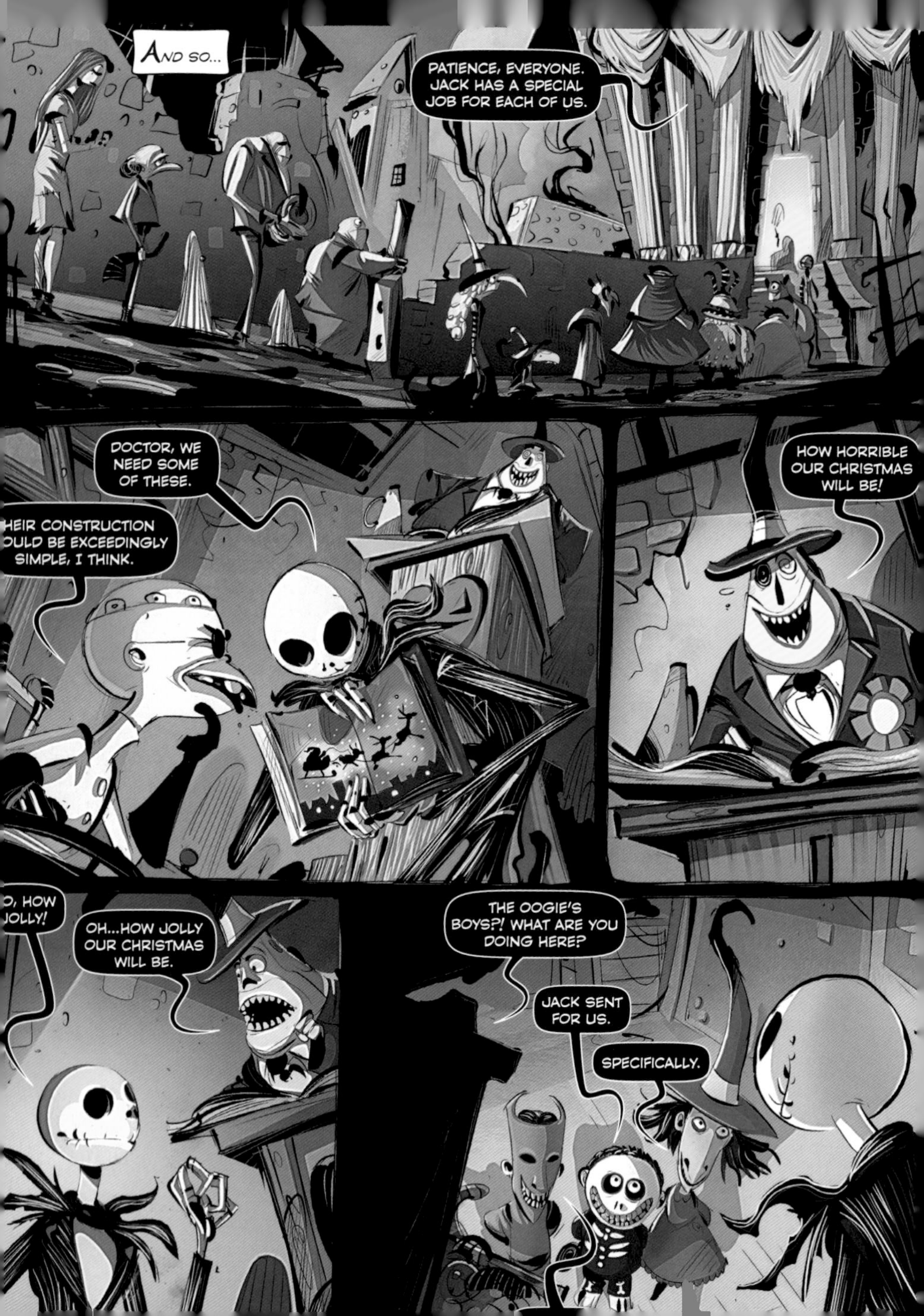

AND SO...
PATIENCE, EVERYONE. JACK HAS A SPECIAL JOB FOR EACH OF US.
DOCTOR, WE NEED SOME OF THESE.
HEIR CONSTRUCTION OULD BE EXCEEDINGLY SIMPLE, I THINK.
HOW HORRIBLE OUR CHRISTMAS WILL BE!
O, HOW JOLLY!
OH...HOW JOLLY OUR CHRISTMAS WILL BE.
THE OOGIE'S BOYS?! WHAT ARE YOU DOING HERE?
JACK SENT FOR US.
SPECIFICALLY.

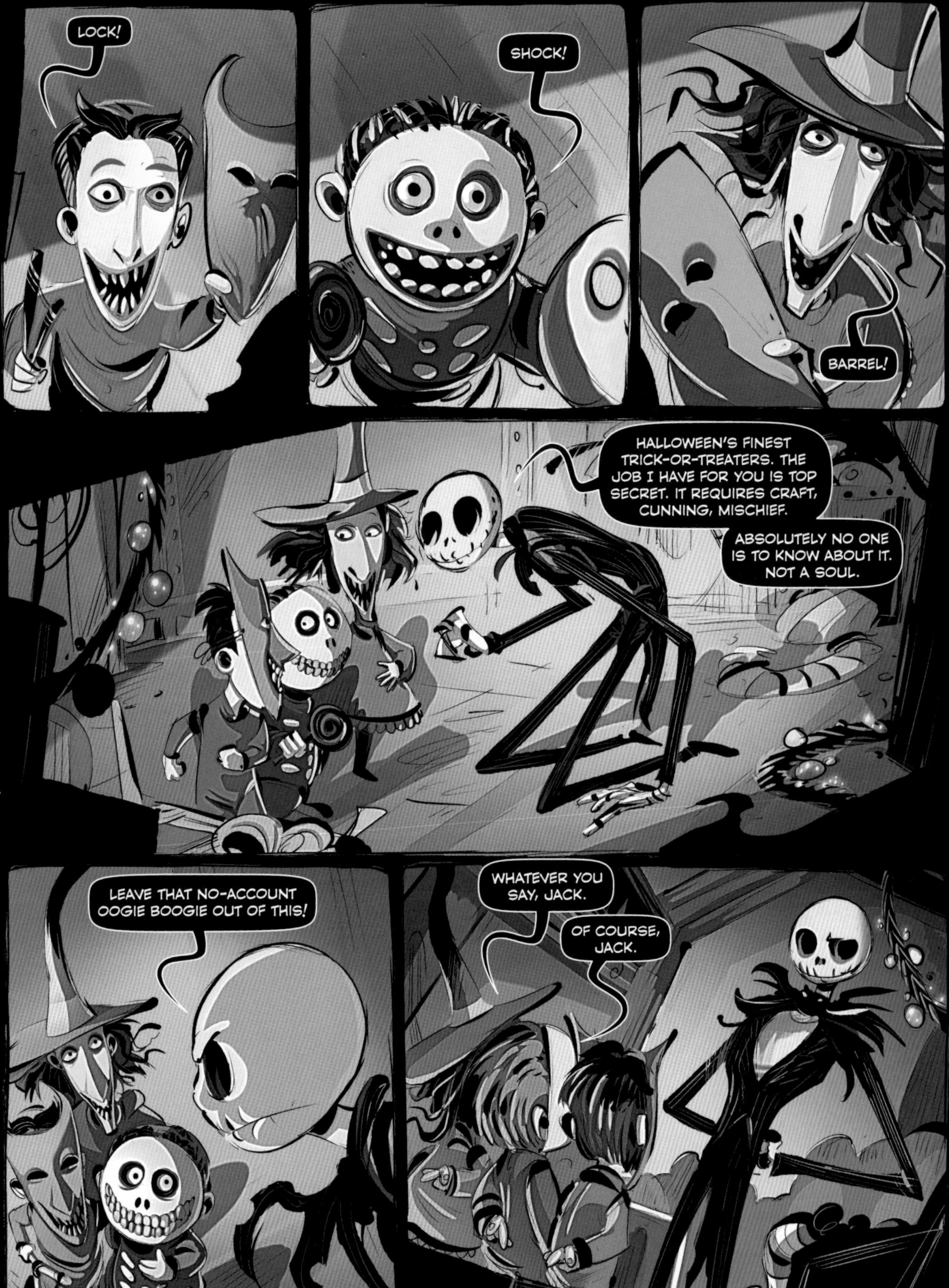
LOCK!
SHOCK!
BARREL!
HALLOWEEN'S FINEST TRICK-OR-TREATERS. THE JOB I HAVE FOR YOU IS TOP SECRET. IT REQUIRES CRAFT, CUNNING, MISCHIEF.
ABSOLUTELY NO ONE IS TO KNOW ABOUT IT. NOT A SOUL.
LEAVE THAT NO-ACCOUNT OOGIE BOOGIE OUT OF THIS!
WHATEVER YOU SAY, JACK.
OF COURSE, JACK.

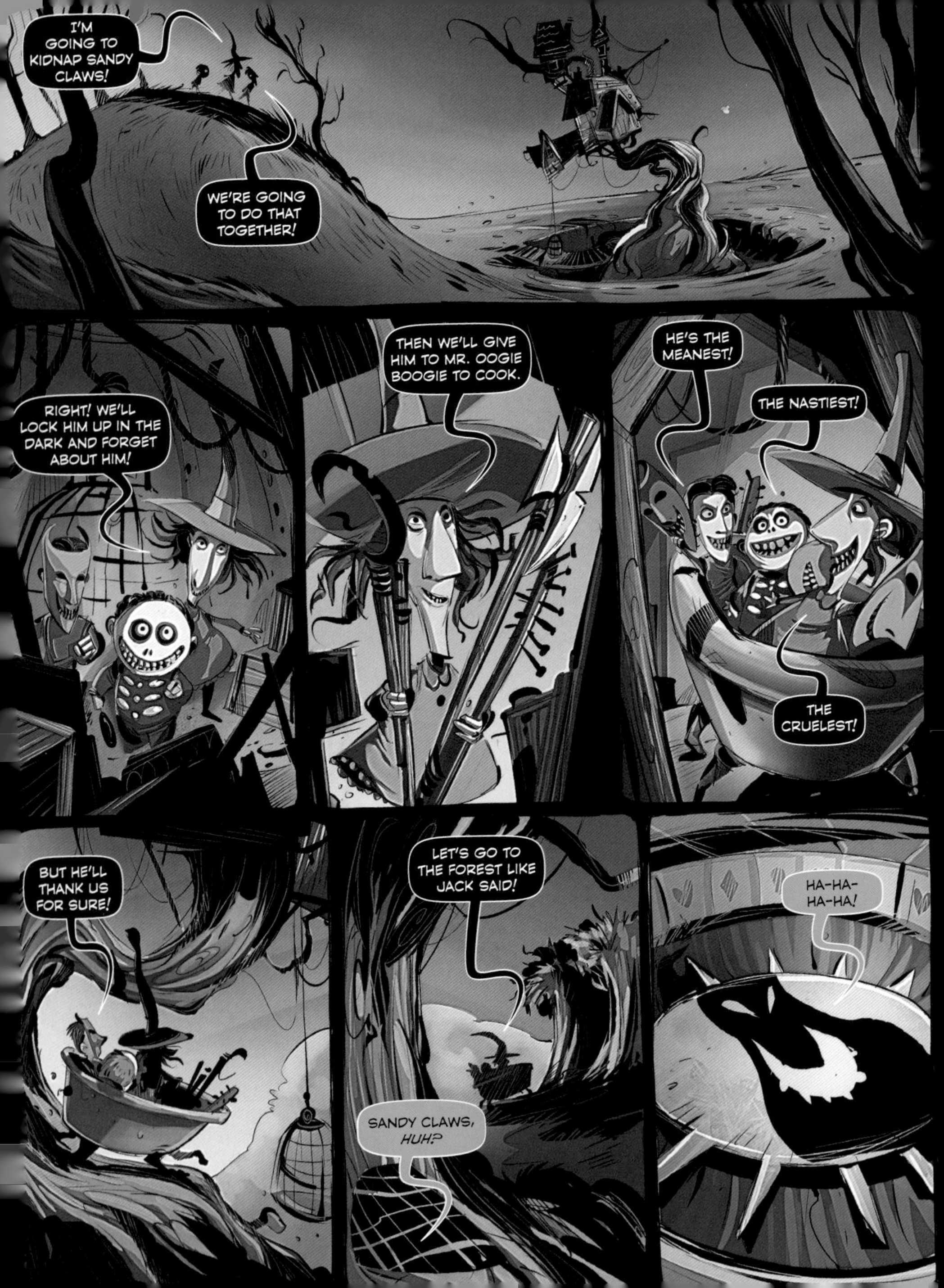
I'M GOING TO KIDNAP SANDY CLAWS!
WE'RE GOING TO DO THAT TOGETHER!
RIGHT! WE'LL LOCK HIM UP IN THE DARK AND FORGET ABOUT HIM!
THEN WE'LL GIVE HIM TO MR. OOGIE BOOGIE TO COOK.
HE'S THE MEANEST!
THE NASTIEST!
THE CRUELEST!
BUT HE'LL THANK US FOR SURE!
LET'S GO TO THE FOREST LIKE JACK SAID!
SANDY CLAWS, *HUH?*
HA-HA-HA-HA!

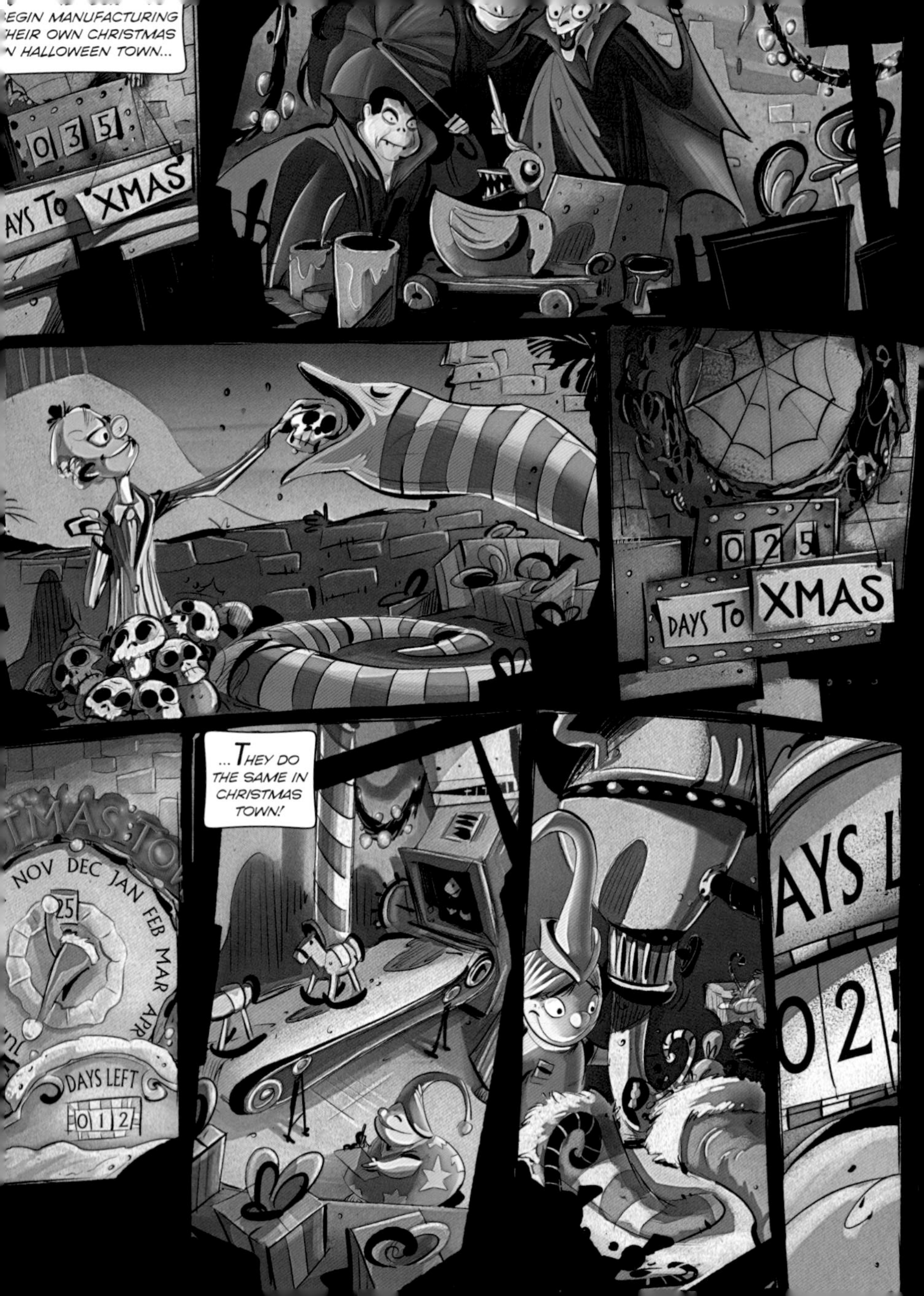

EGIN MANUFACTURING
THEIR OWN CHRISTMAS
N HALLOWEEN TOWN...
035
AYS TO XMAS
025
DAYS TO XMAS
NOV DEC JAN FEB MAR APR
25
DAYS LEFT
012
...THEY DO THE SAME IN CHRISTMAS TOWN!
AYS L
02

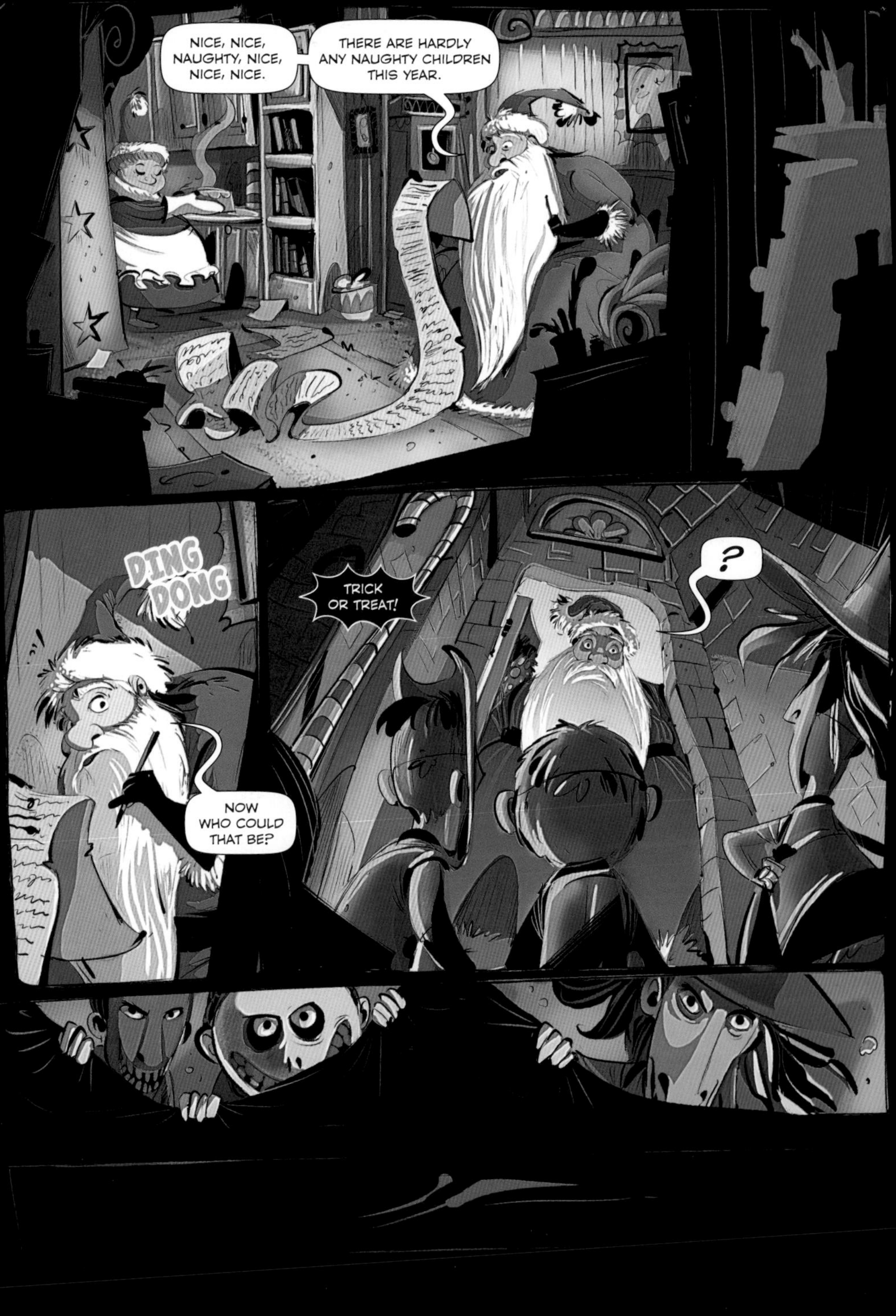
NICE, NICE, NAUGHTY, NICE, NICE, NICE.
THERE ARE HARDLY ANY NAUGHTY CHILDREN THIS YEAR.
DING DONG
NOW WHO COULD THAT BE?
TRICK OR TREAT!
?

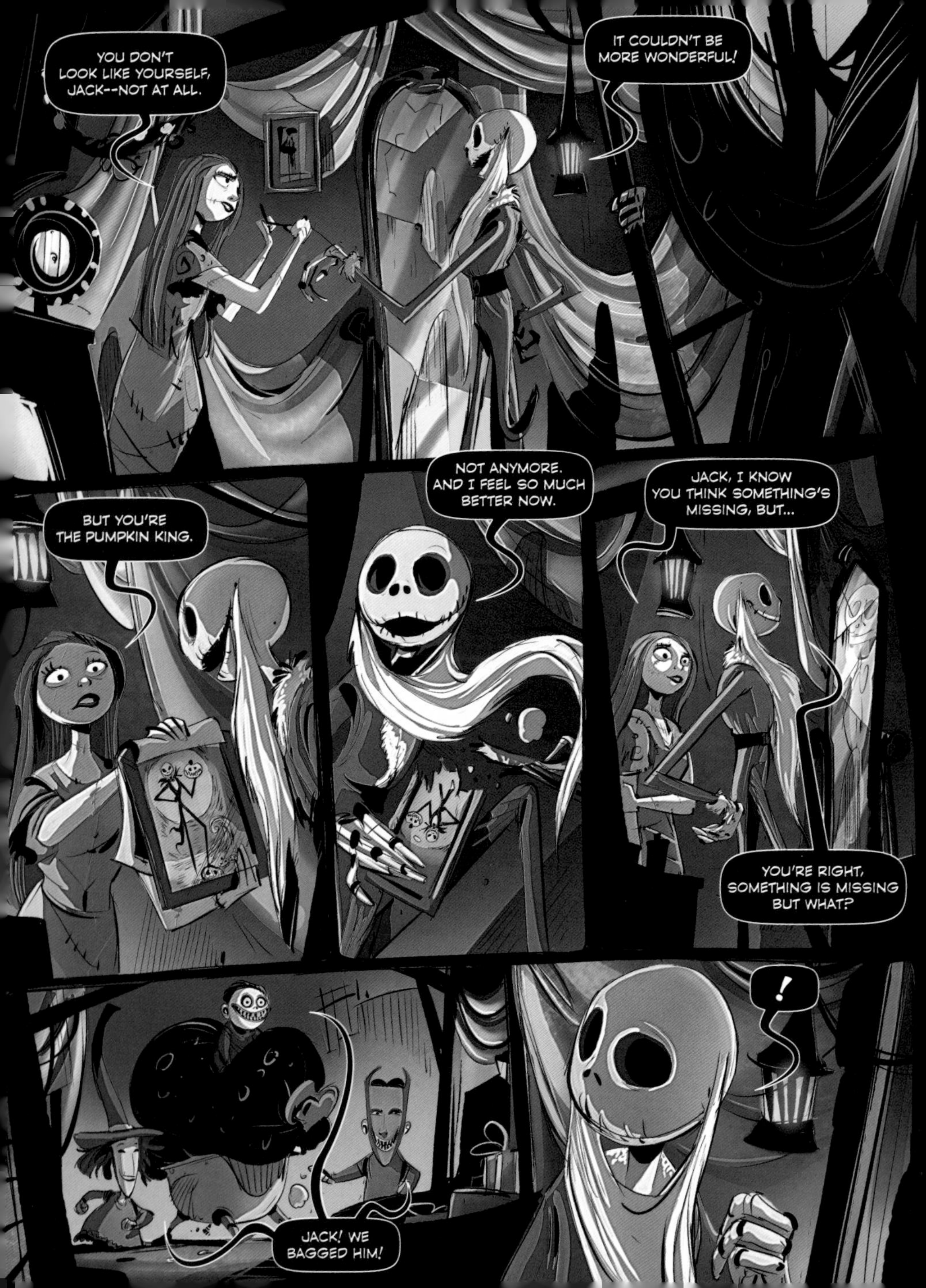
YOU DON'T LOOK LIKE YOURSELF, JACK--NOT AT ALL.
IT COULDN'T BE MORE WONDERFUL!
BUT YOU'RE THE PUMPKIN KING.
NOT ANYMORE. AND I FEEL SO MUCH BETTER NOW.
JACK, I KNOW YOU THINK SOMETHING'S MISSING, BUT...
YOU'RE RIGHT, SOMETHING IS MISSING BUT WHAT?
JACK! WE BAGGED HIM!
!

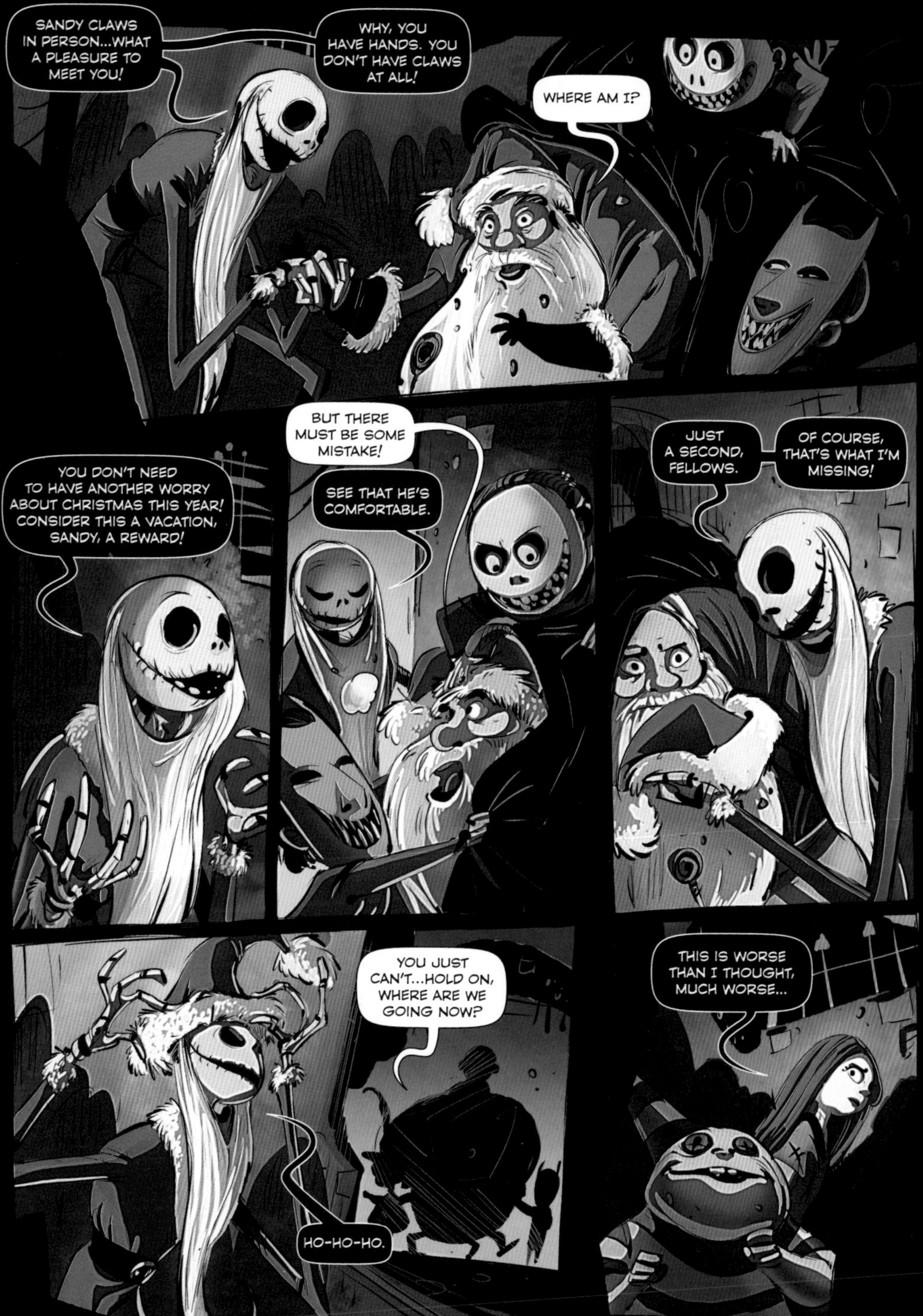
SANDY CLAWS IN PERSON...WHAT A PLEASURE TO MEET YOU!
WHY, YOU HAVE HANDS. YOU DON'T HAVE CLAWS AT ALL!
WHERE AM I?
YOU DON'T NEED TO HAVE ANOTHER WORRY ABOUT CHRISTMAS THIS YEAR! CONSIDER THIS A VACATION, SANDY, A REWARD!
BUT THERE MUST BE SOME MISTAKE!
SEE THAT HE'S COMFORTABLE.
JUST A SECOND, FELLOWS.
OF COURSE, THAT'S WHAT I'M MISSING!
YOU JUST CAN'T...HOLD ON, WHERE ARE WE GOING NOW?
HO-HO-HO.
THIS IS WORSE THAN I THOUGHT, MUCH WORSE...

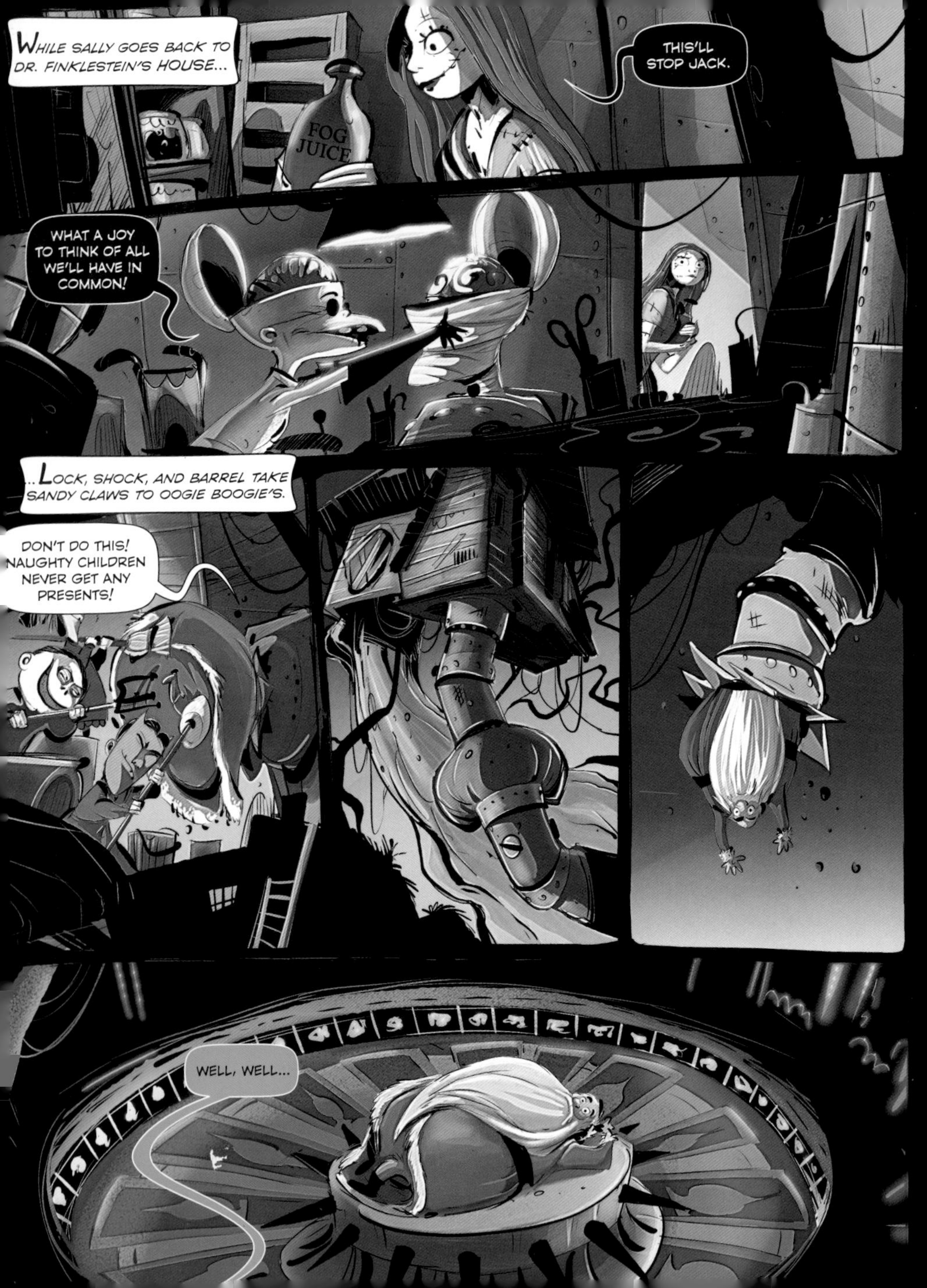

WHILE SALLY GOES BACK TO DR. FINKLESTEIN'S HOUSE...
FOG JUICE
THIS'LL STOP JACK.
WHAT A JOY TO THINK OF ALL WE'LL HAVE IN COMMON!
...LOCK, SHOCK, AND BARREL TAKE SANDY CLAWS TO OOGIE BOOGIE'S.
DON'T DO THIS! NAUGHTY CHILDREN NEVER GET ANY PRESENTS!
WELL, WELL...

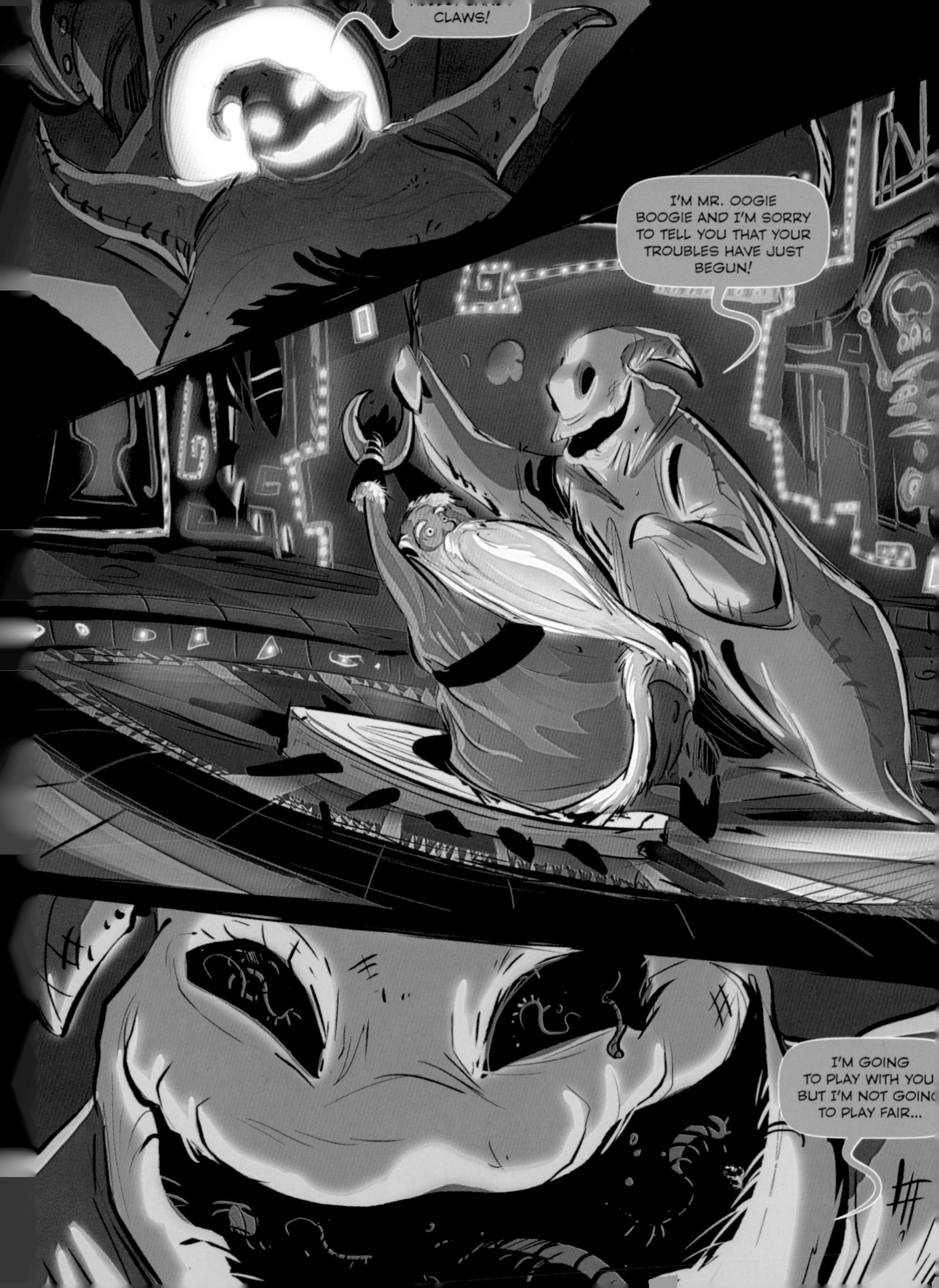

CLAWS!
I'M MR. OOGIE BOOGIE AND I'M SORRY TO TELL YOU THAT YOUR TROUBLES HAVE JUST BEGUN!
I'M GOING TO PLAY WITH YOU BUT I'M NOT GOIN TO PLAY FAIR...

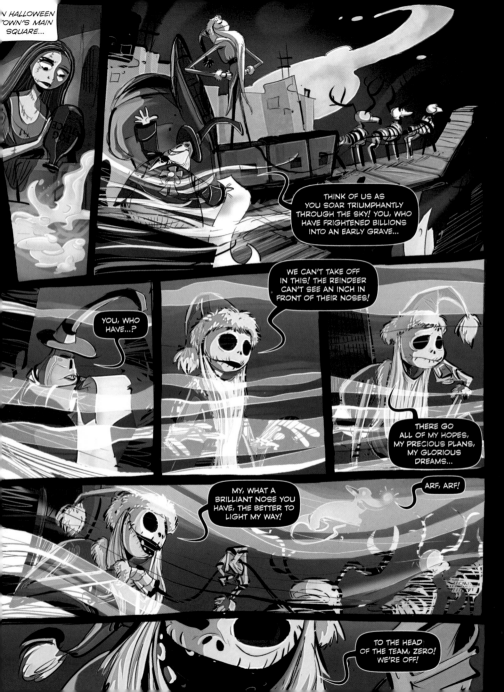

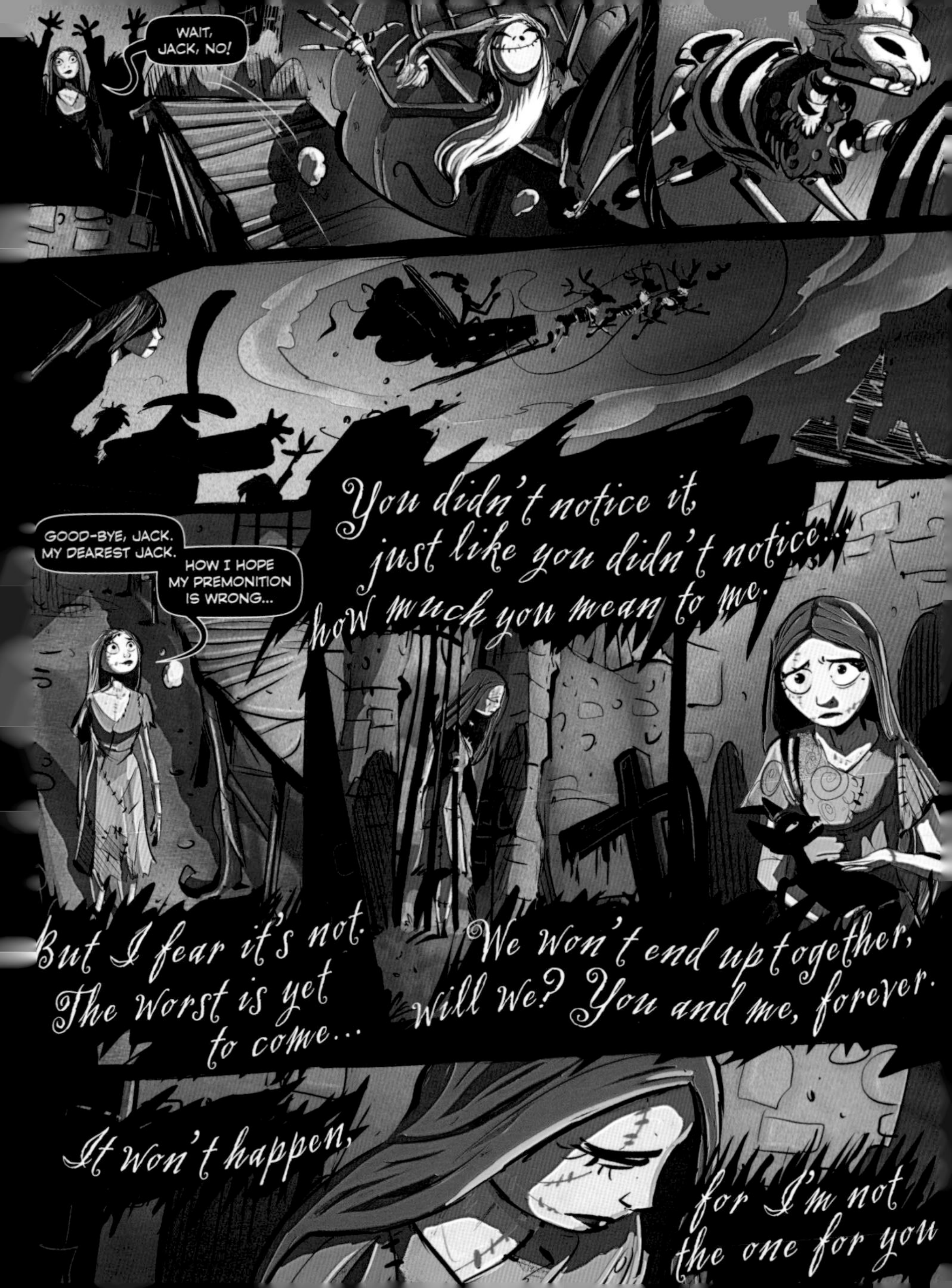
WAIT, JACK, NO!
GOOD-BYE, JACK. MY DEAREST JACK.
HOW I HOPE MY PREMONITION IS WRONG...
You didn't notice it just like you didn't notice... how much you mean to me.
But I fear it's not. The worst is yet to come...
We won't end up together, will we? You and me, forever.
It won't happen,
for I'm not the one for you

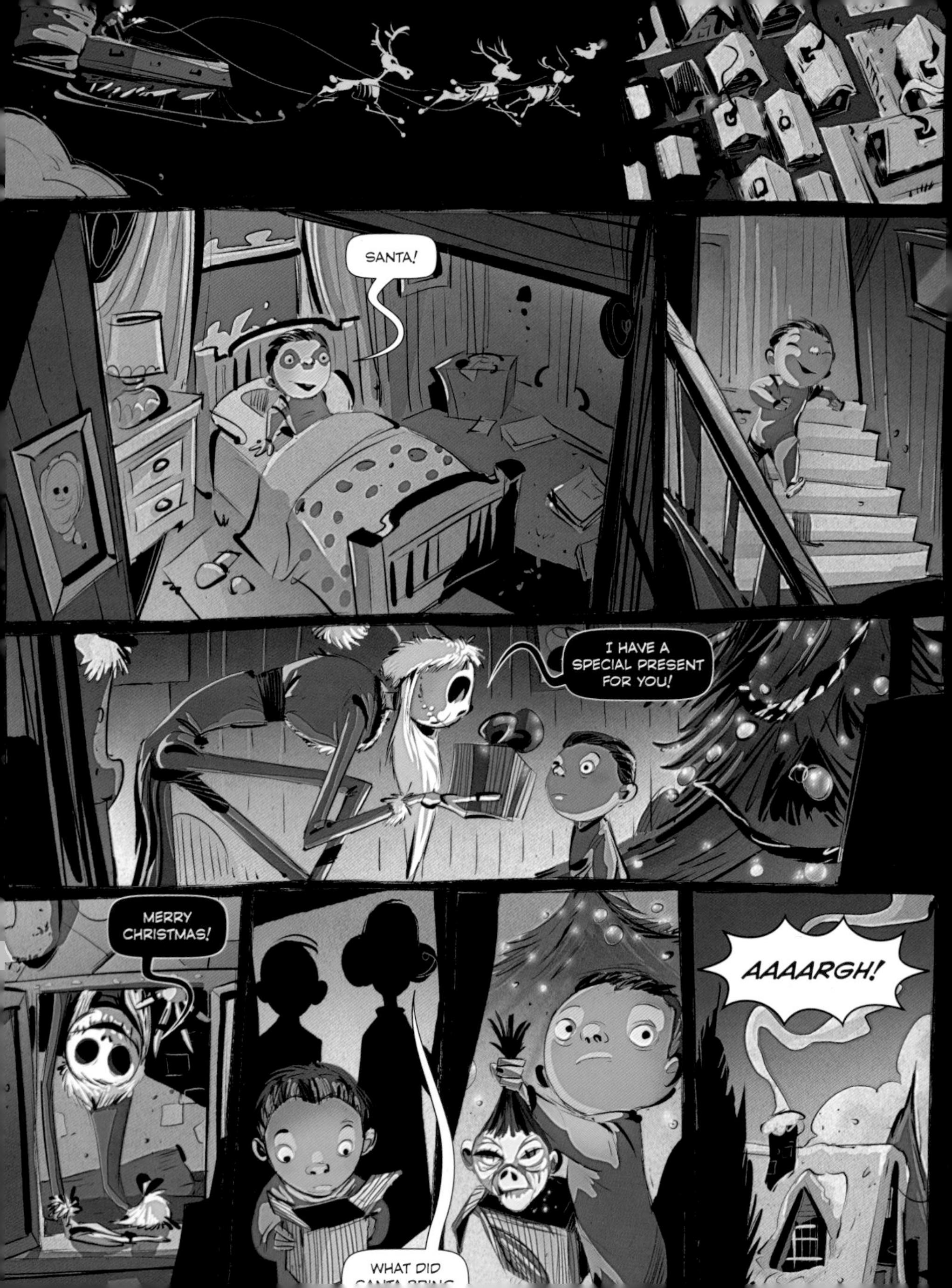
SANTA!
I HAVE A SPECIAL PRESENT FOR YOU!
MERRY CHRISTMAS!
WHAT DID
AAAARGH!

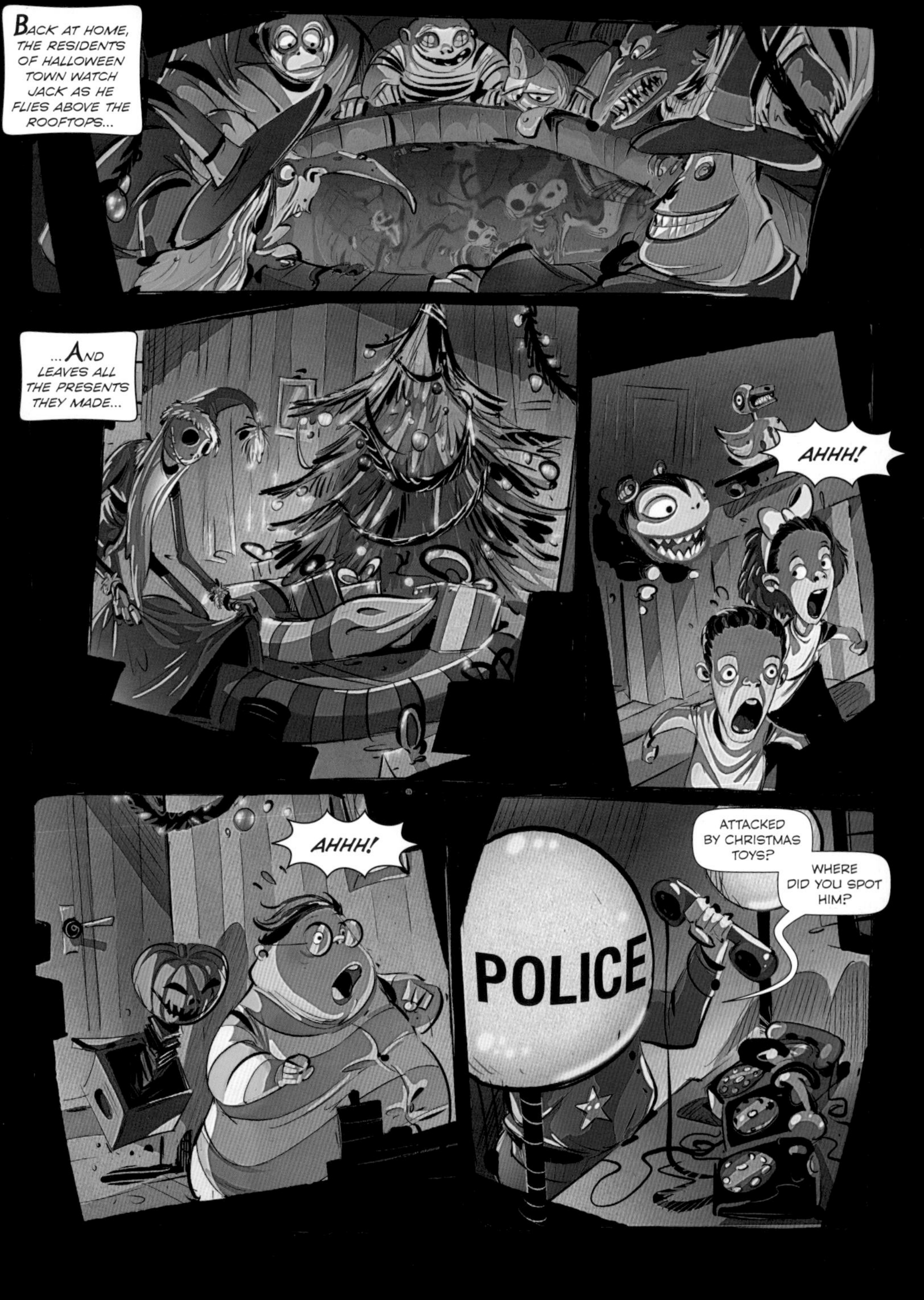
BACK AT HOME, THE RESIDENTS OF HALLOWEEN TOWN WATCH JACK AS HE FLIES ABOVE THE ROOFTOPS...
...AND LEAVES ALL THE PRESENTS THEY MADE...
AHHH!
AHHH!
POLICE
ATTACKED BY CHRISTMAS TOYS?
WHERE DID YOU SPOT HIM?

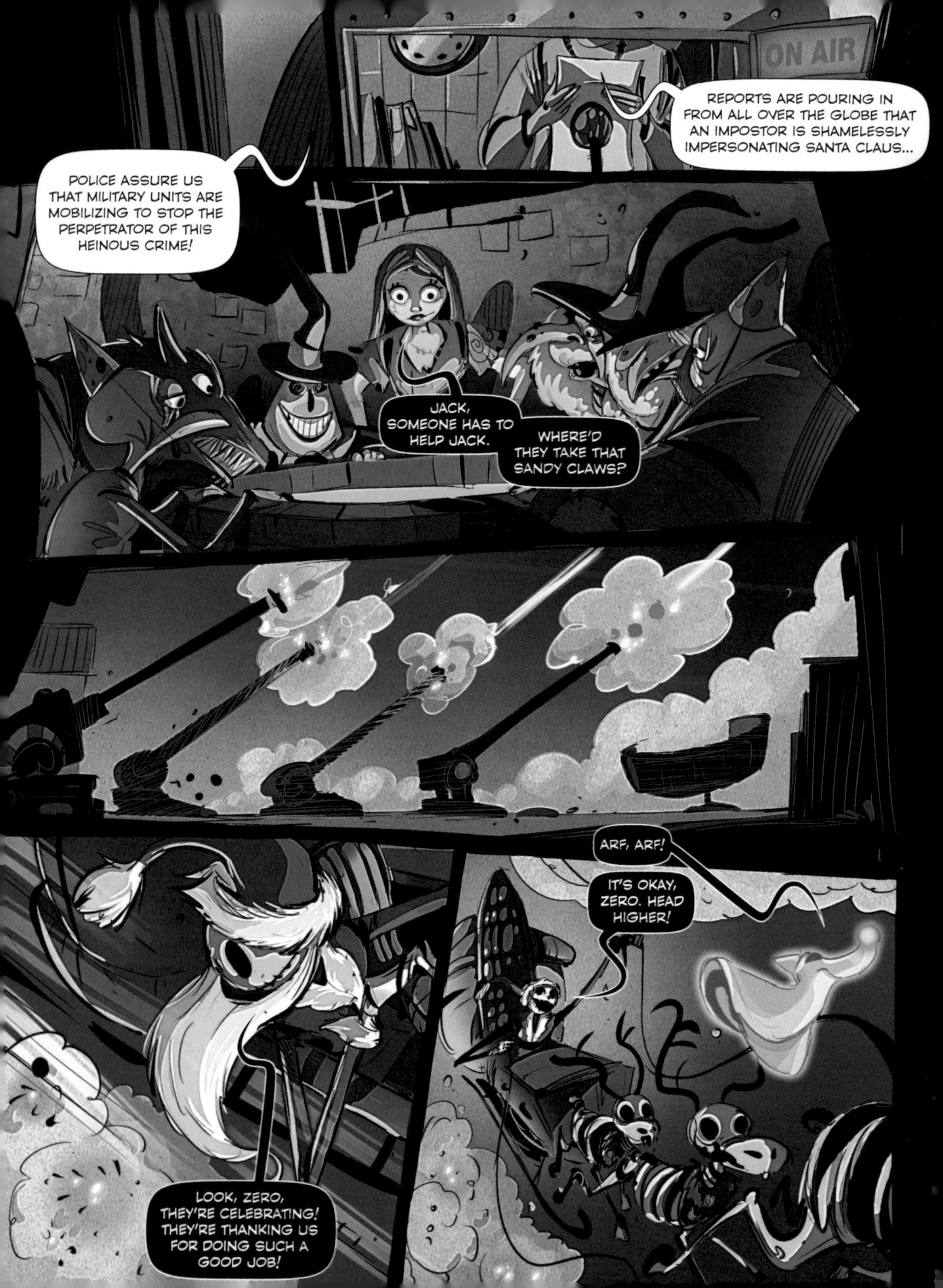
ON AIR
REPORTS ARE POURING IN FROM ALL OVER THE GLOBE THAT AN IMPOSTOR IS SHAMELESSLY IMPERSONATING SANTA CLAUS...
POLICE ASSURE US THAT MILITARY UNITS ARE MOBILIZING TO STOP THE PERPETRATOR OF THIS HEINOUS CRIME!
JACK, SOMEONE HAS TO HELP JACK.
WHERE'D THEY TAKE THAT SANDY CLAWS?
LOOK, ZERO, THEY'RE CELEBRATING! THEY'RE THANKING US FOR DOING SUCH A GOOD JOB!
ARF, ARF!
IT'S OKAY, ZERO. HEAD HIGHER!

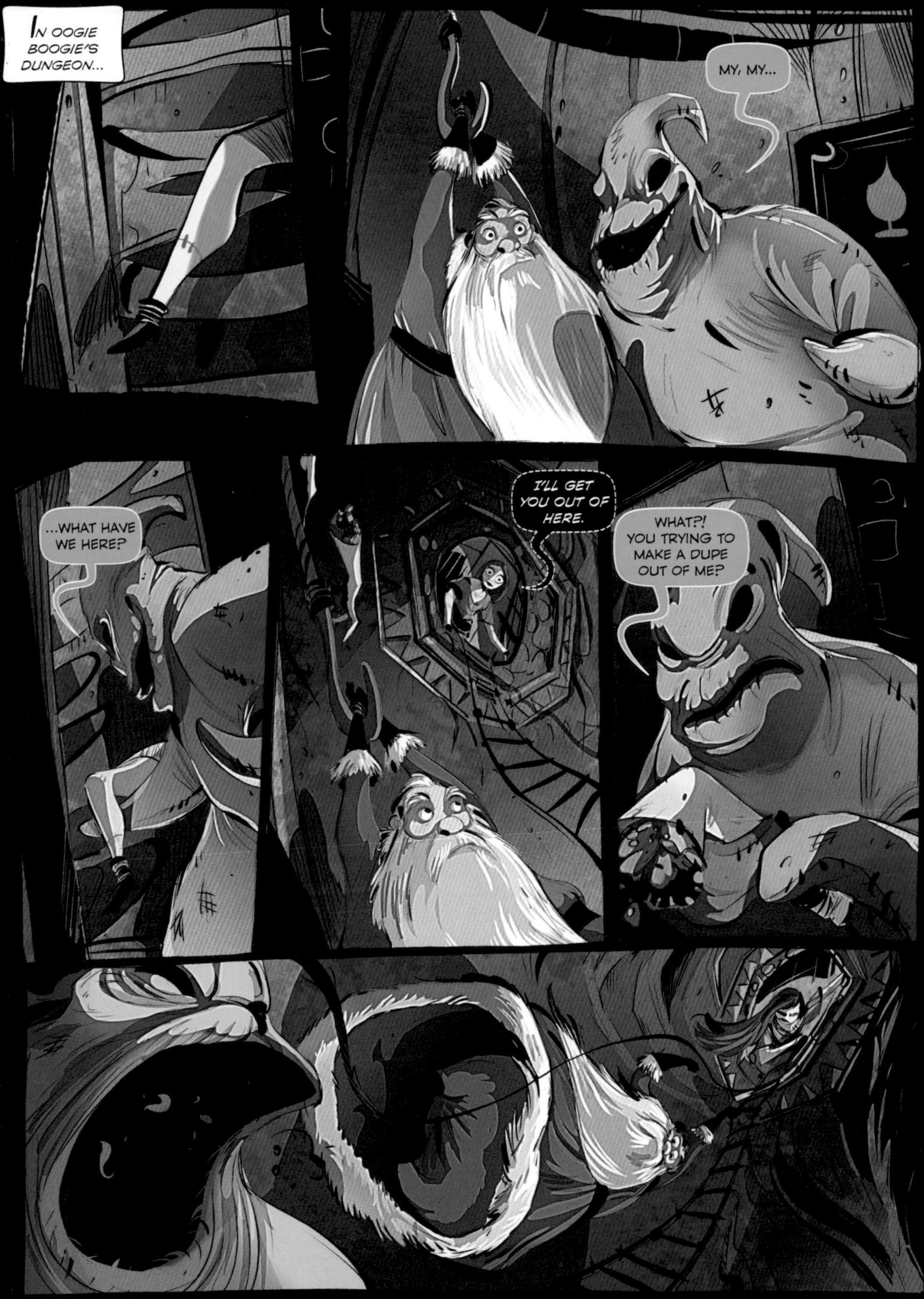

IN OOGIE BOOGIE'S DUNGEON...
MY, MY...
...WHAT HAVE WE HERE?
I'LL GET YOU OUT OF HERE.
WHAT?! YOU TRYING TO MAKE A DUPE OUT OF ME?

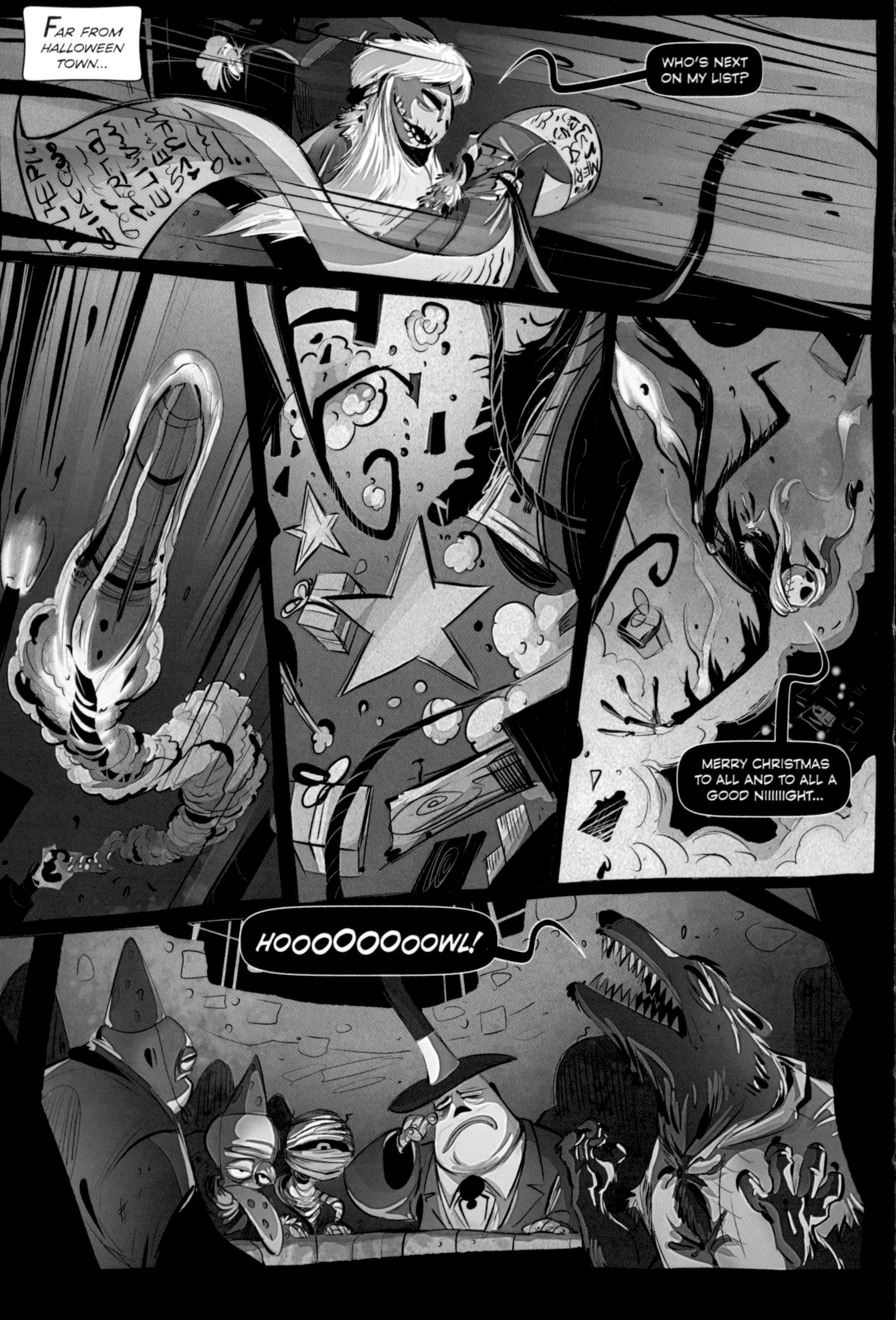
FAR FROM HALLOWEEN TOWN...
WHO'S NEXT ON MY LIST?
MERRY CHRISTMAS TO ALL AND TO ALL A GOOD NIIIIIIGHT...
HOOOOOOOOOWL!

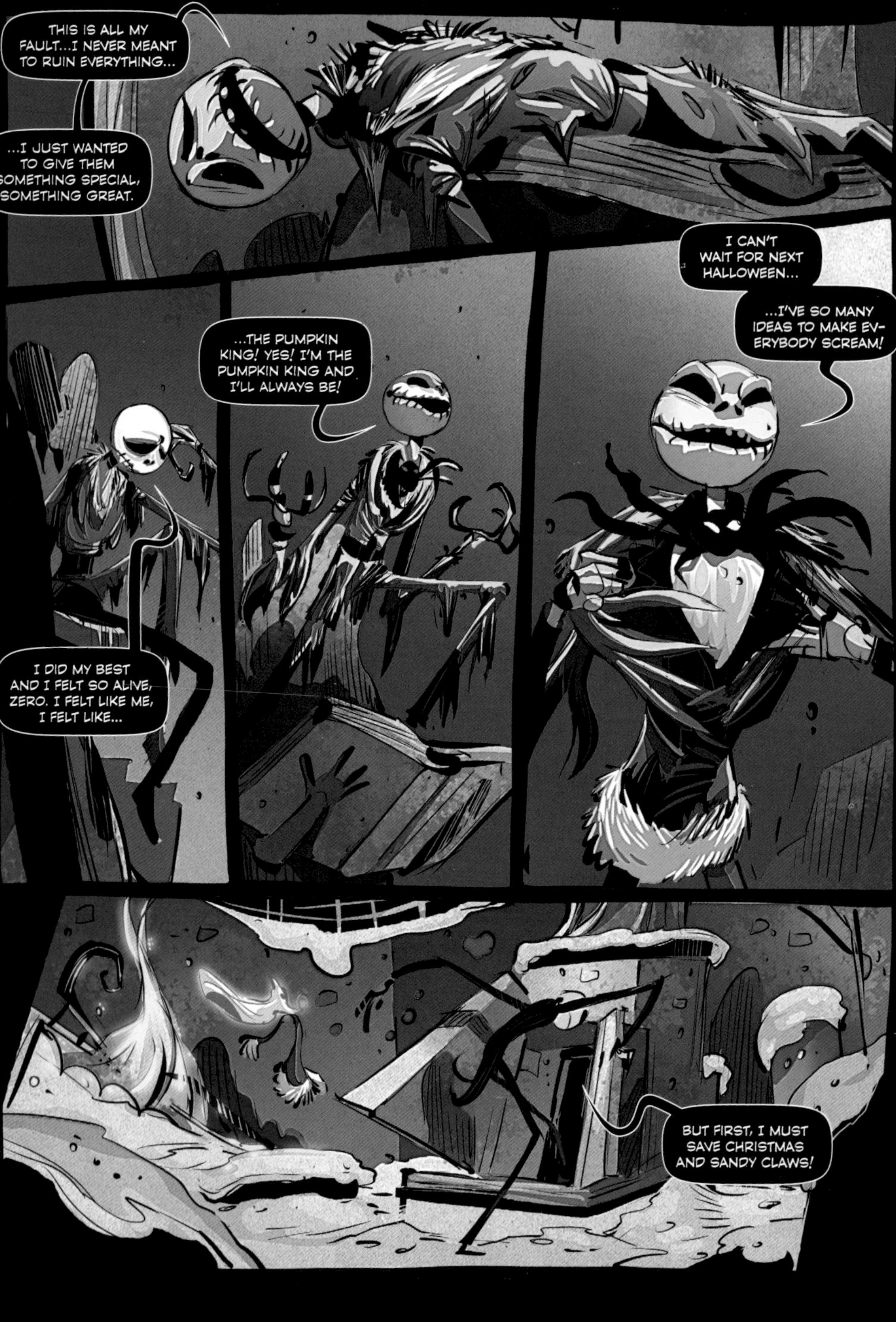
THIS IS ALL MY FAULT...I NEVER MEANT TO RUIN EVERYTHING...
...I JUST WANTED TO GIVE THEM SOMETHING SPECIAL, SOMETHING GREAT.
I DID MY BEST AND I FELT SO ALIVE, ZERO. I FELT LIKE ME, I FELT LIKE...
...THE PUMPKIN KING! YES! I'M THE PUMPKIN KING AND I'LL ALWAYS BE!
I CAN'T WAIT FOR NEXT HALLOWEEN...
...I'VE SO MANY IDEAS TO MAKE EV-ERYBODY SCREAM!
BUT FIRST, I MUST SAVE CHRISTMAS AND SANDY CLAWS!

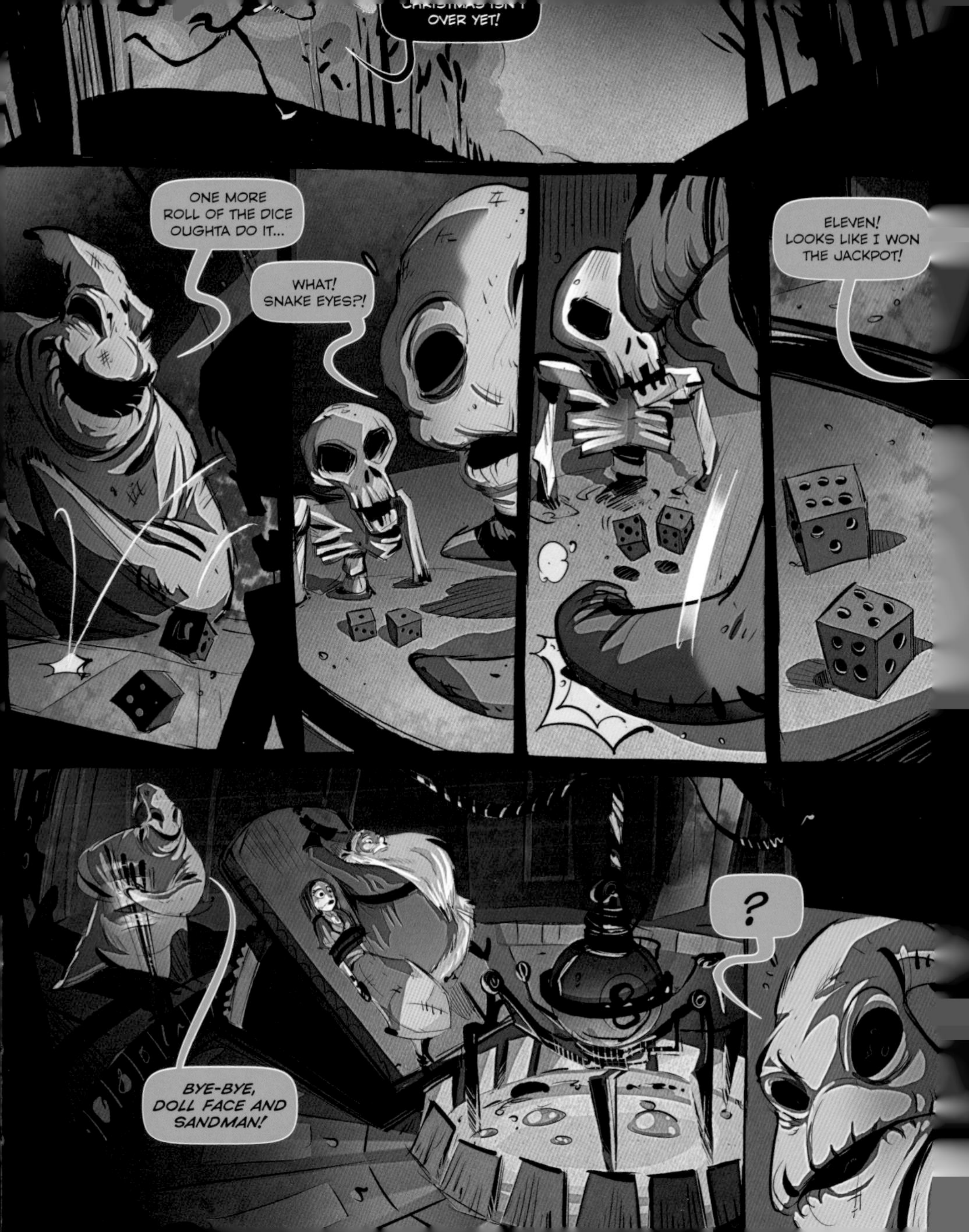
OVER YET!
ONE MORE ROLL OF THE DICE OUGHTA DO IT...
WHAT! SNAKE EYES?!
ELEVEN! LOOKS LIKE I WON THE JACKPOT!
BYE-BYE, DOLL FACE AND SANDMAN!
?

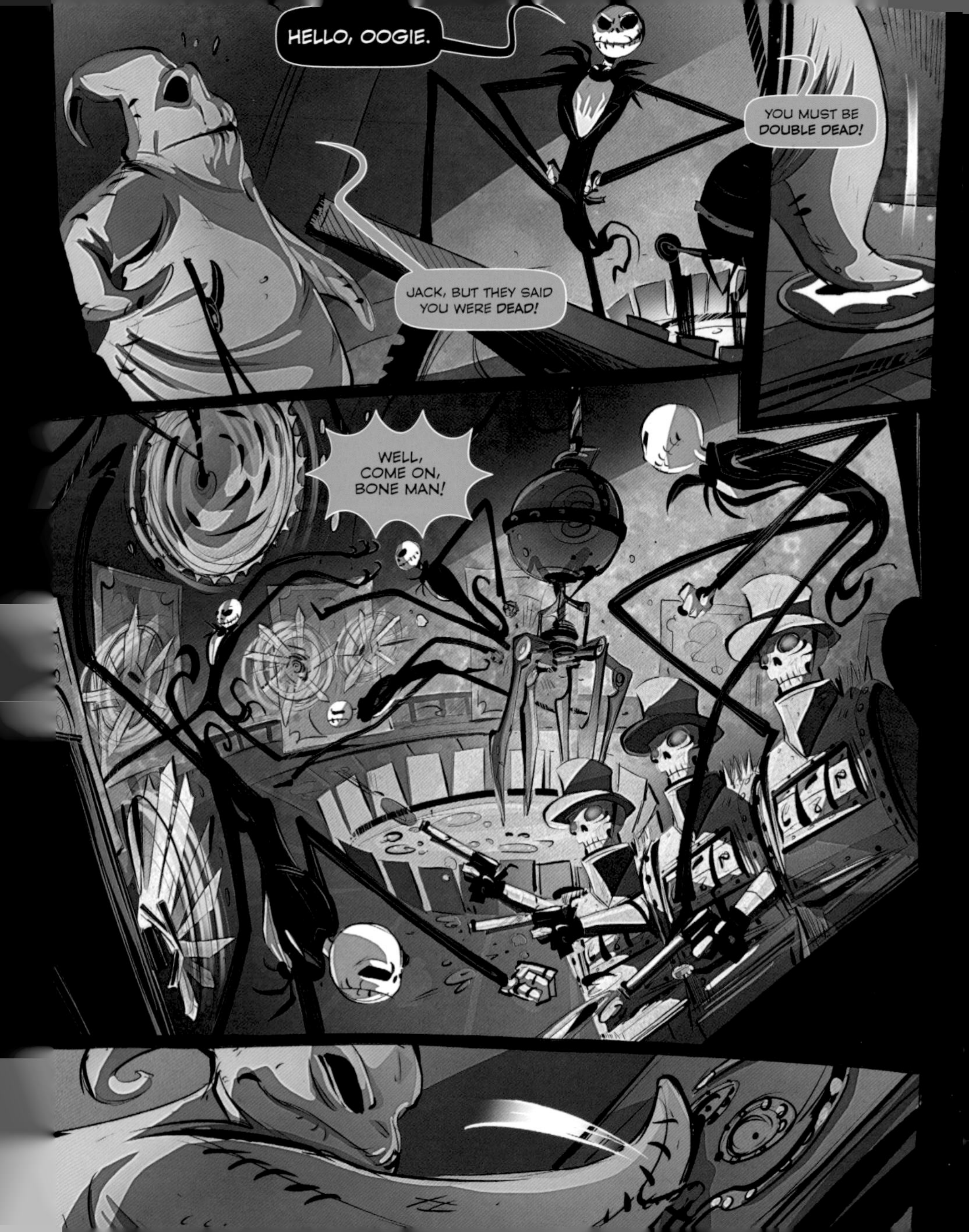
HELLO, OOGIE.
JACK, BUT THEY SAID YOU WERE DEAD!
YOU MUST BE DOUBLE DEAD!
WELL, COME ON, BONE MAN!

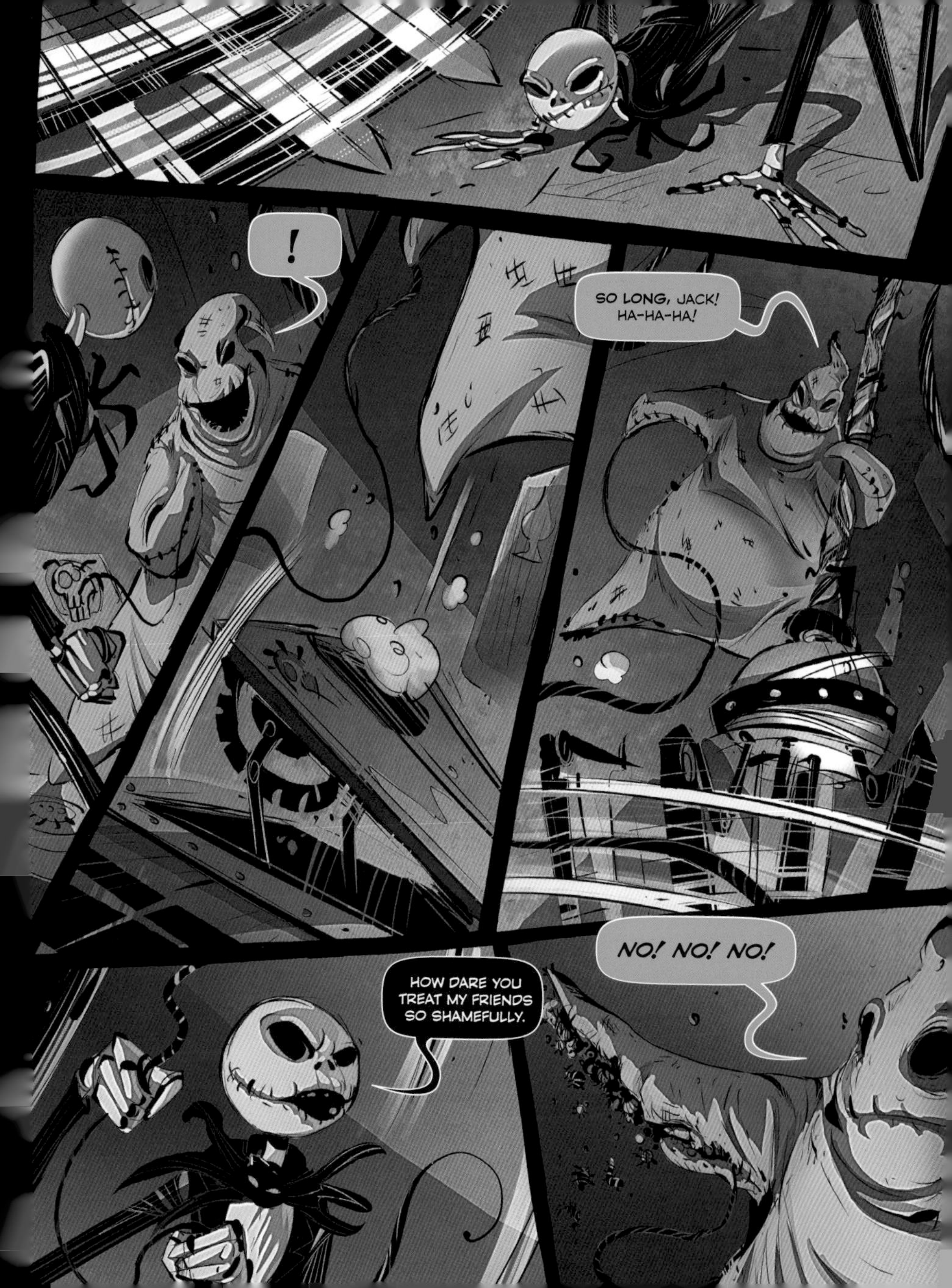
!
SO LONG, JACK! HA-HA-HA!
HOW DARE YOU TREAT MY FRIENDS SO SHAMEFULLY.
NO! NO! NO!

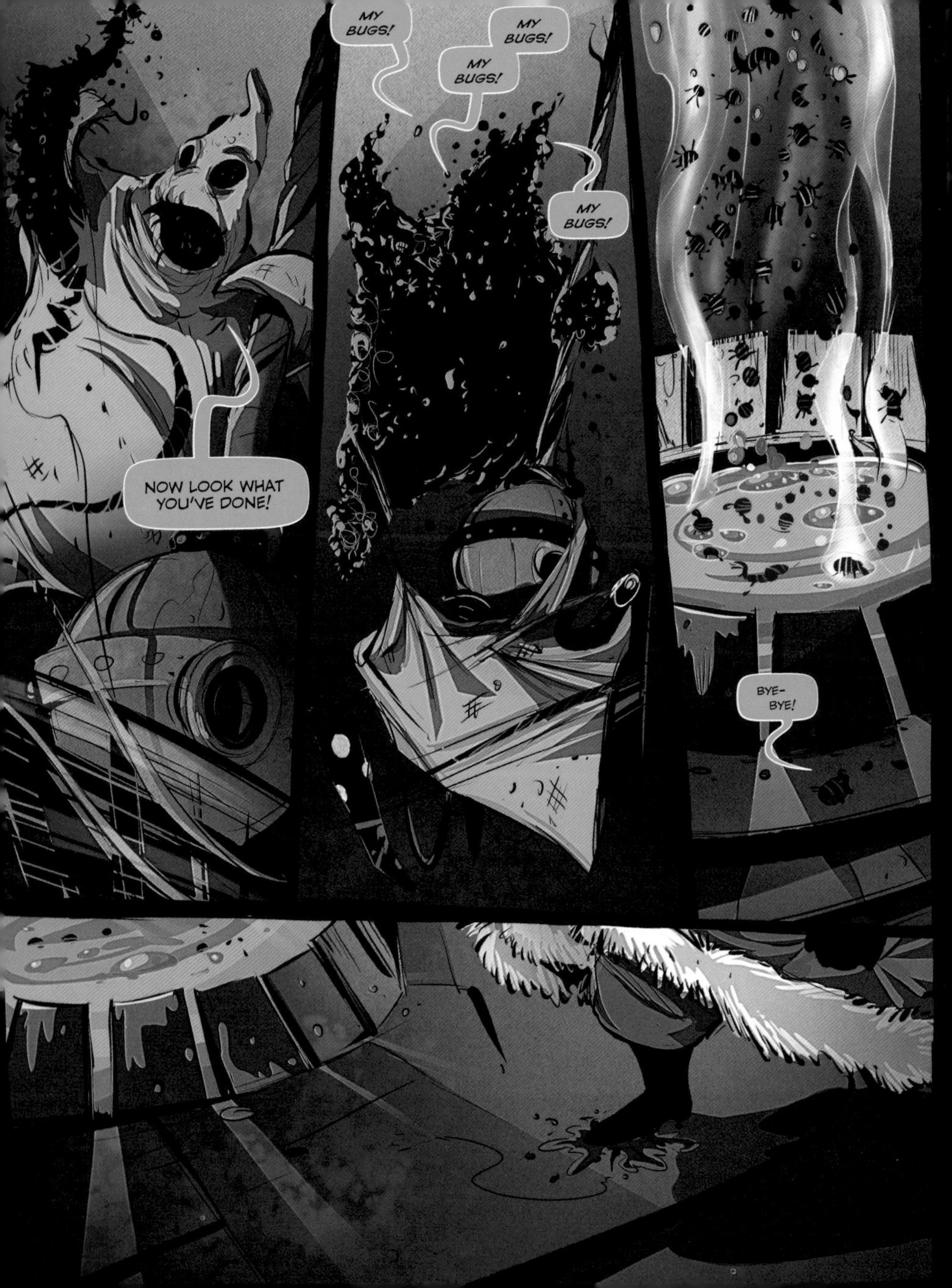
NOW LOOK WHAT YOU'VE DONE!
MY BUGS!
MY BUGS!
MY BUGS!
MY BUGS!
BYE-BYE!

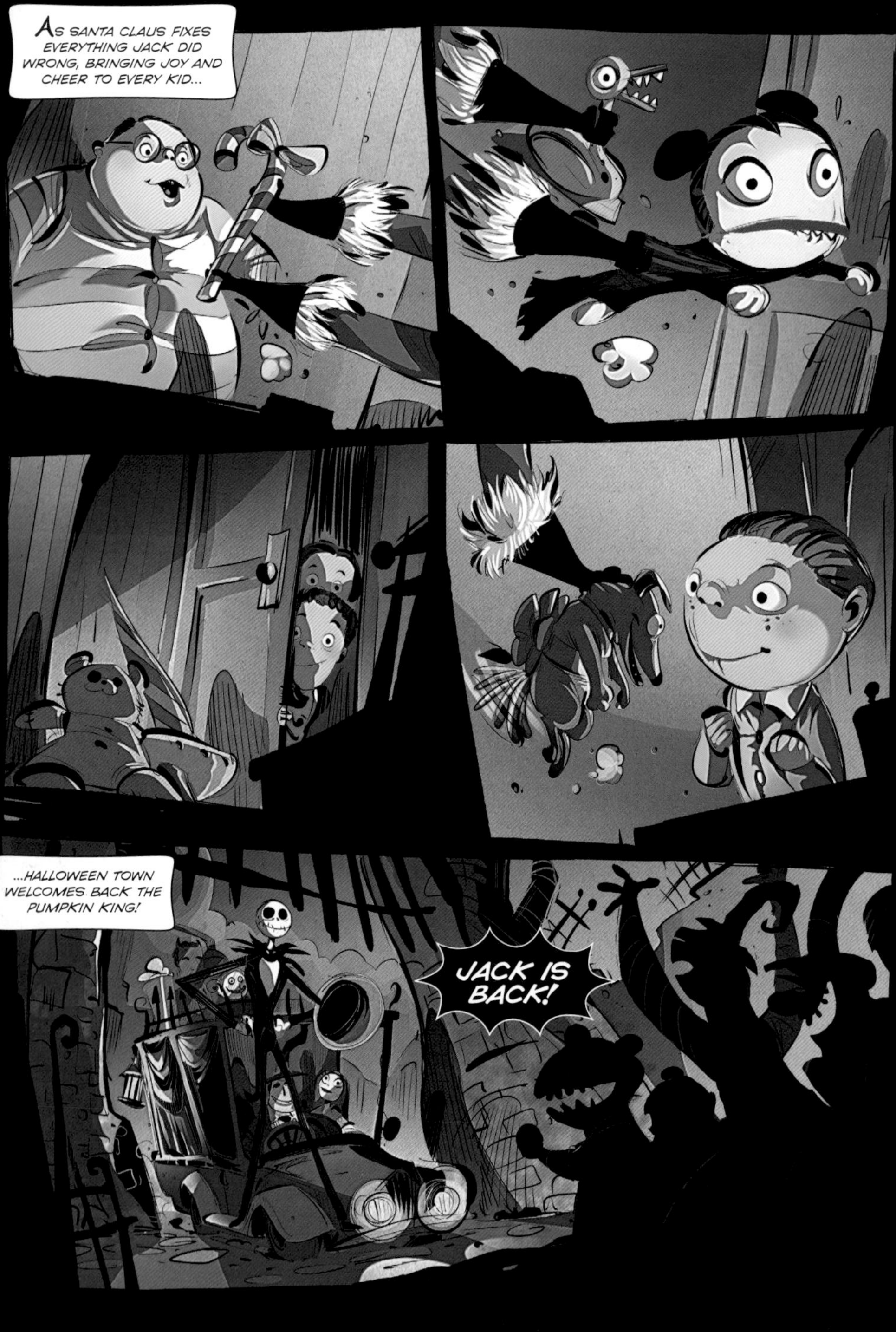
As santa claus fixes everything Jack did wrong, bringing joy and cheer to every kid...
...Halloween town welcomes back the pumpkin king!
JACK IS BACK!

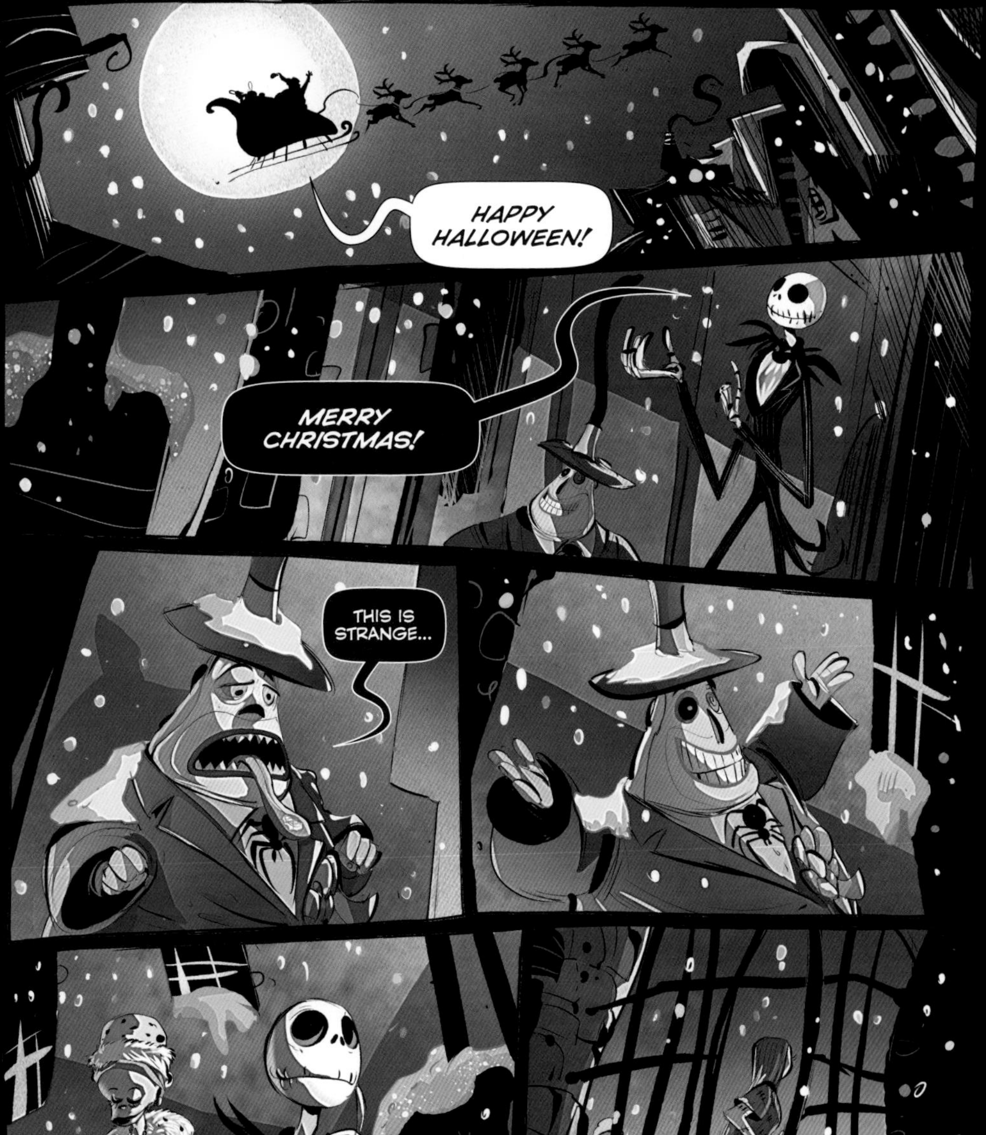
HAPPY HALLOWEEN!
MERRY CHRISTMAS!
THIS IS STRANGE...

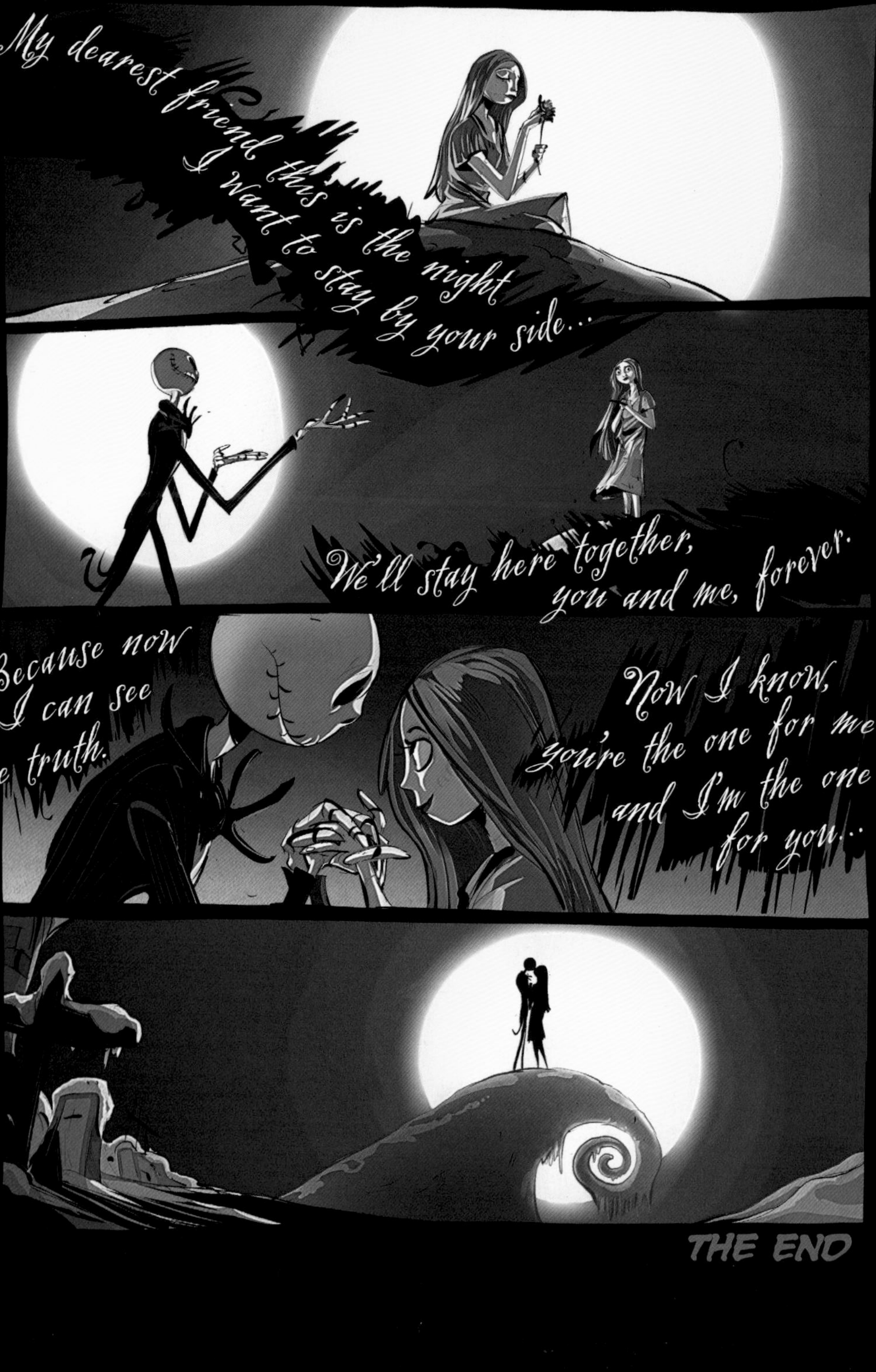

My dearest friend this is the night
I want to stay by your side...
We'll stay here together,
you and me, forever.
Because now I can see the truth.
Now I know, you're the one for me and I'm the one for you...
THE END

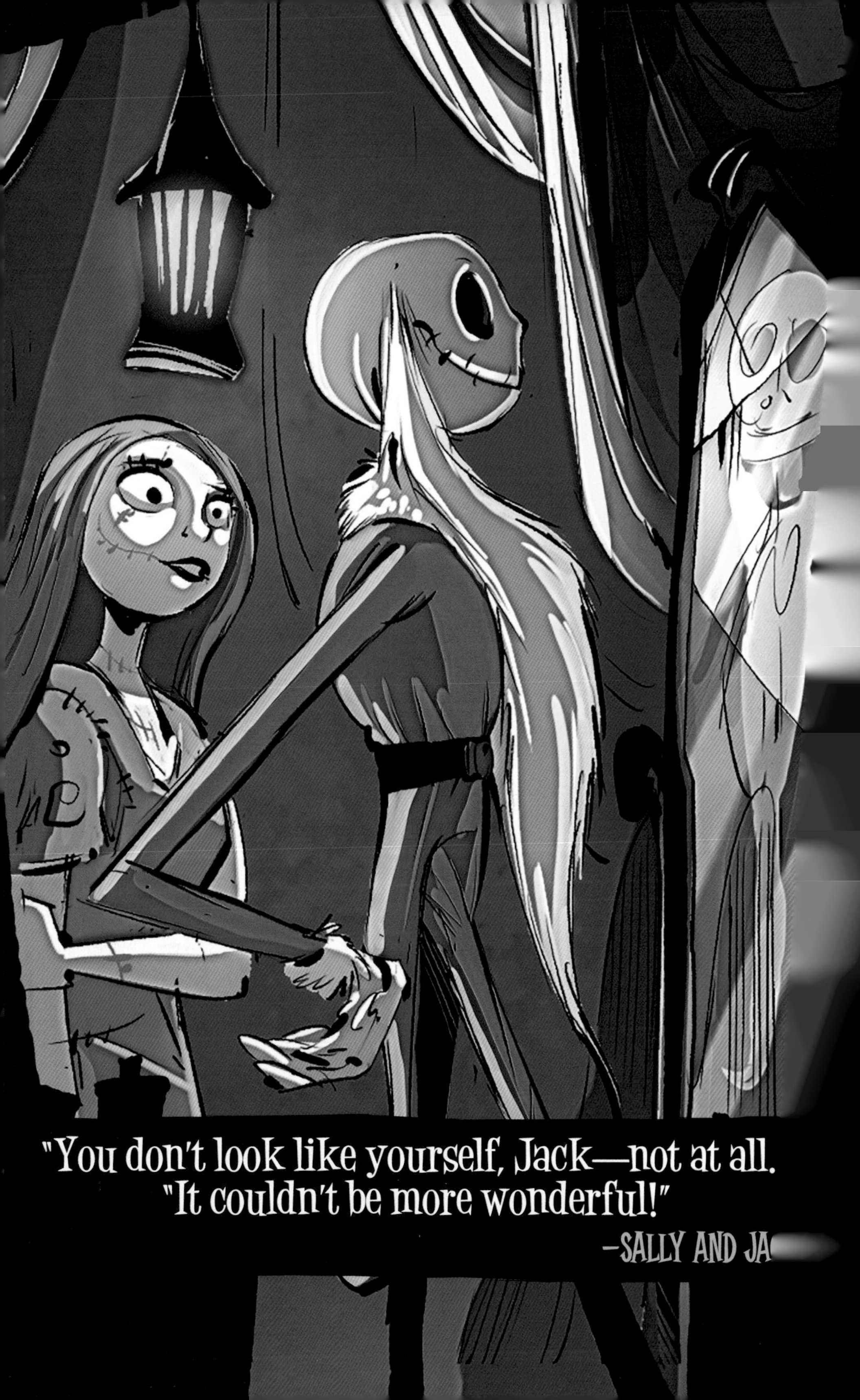

"You don't look like yourself, Jack—not at all.
"It couldn't be more wonderful!"

—SALLY AND JA

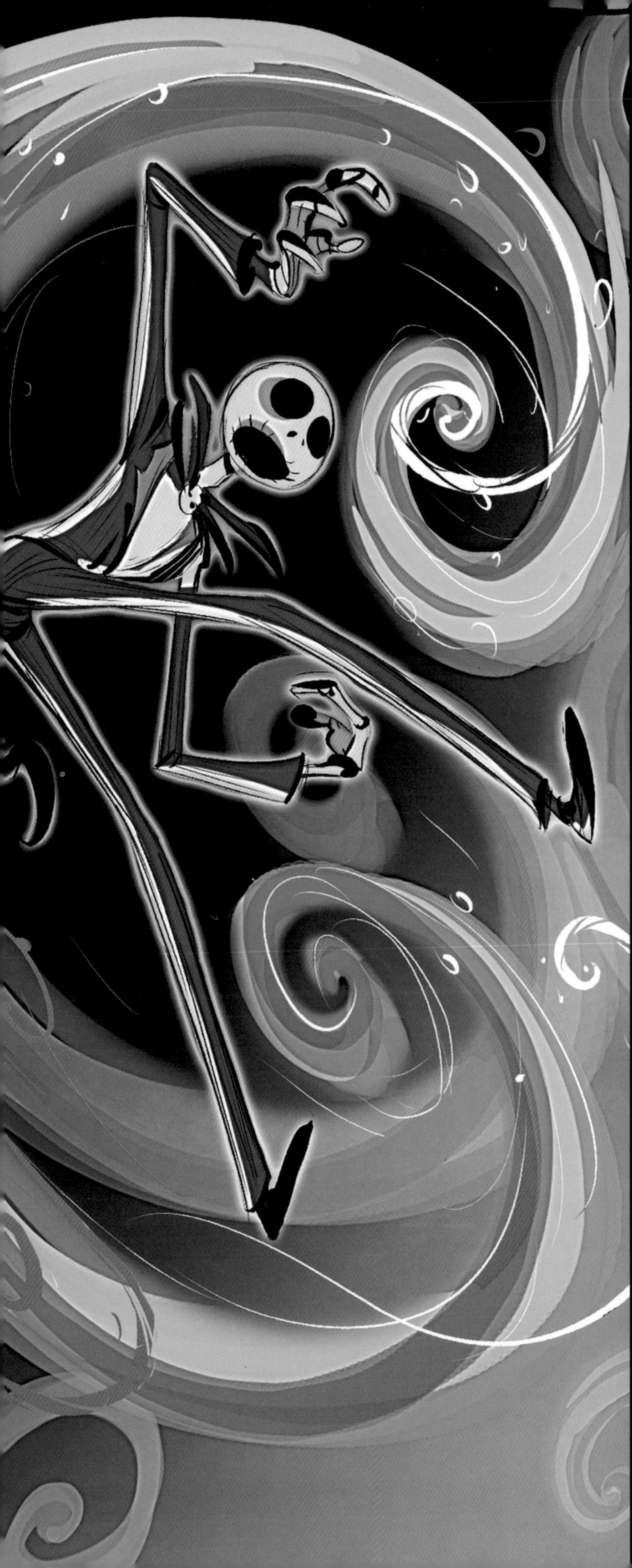

THE GRAPHIC NOVEL

SCRIPT ADAPTATION
Alessandro Ferrari

LAYOUTS, PENCILS & INKS
Massimiliano Narciso

COLOR
Kawaii Studio

LETTERS
Edizioni BD

COVER

LAYOUTS, PENCILS & INKS
Massimiliano Narciso

COLOR
Kawaii Studio

DISNEY PUBLISHING WORLDWIDE
Global Magazines, Comics and Partworks

PUBLISHER
Lynn Waggoner

EDITORIAL TEAM
Bianca Coletti (Director, Magazines), Guido Frazzini (Director, Comics), Stefano Ambrosio (Executive Editor), Carlotta Quattrocolo (Executive Editor), Camilla Vedove (Senior Manager, Editorial Development), Behnoosh Khalili (Senior Editor), Julie Dorris (Senior Editor), Mina Riazi (Assistant Editor), Jonathan Manning (Assistant Editor)

DESIGN
Enrico Soave (Senior Designer)

ART
Ken Shue (VP, Global Art), Roberto Santillo (Creative Director), Marco Ghiglione (Creative Manager), Stefano Attardi (Computer Art Designer) Manny Mederos (Senior Illustration Manager, Comics & Magazines)

PORTFOLIO MANAGEMENT
Olivia Ciancarelli (Director)

BUSINESS & MARKETING
Mariantonietta Galla (Marketing Manager), Virpi Korhonen (Editorial Manager)

GRAPHIC DESIGN
Chris Dickey

SPECIAL THANKS
Tim Burton, Dominique Flynn, Dale Kennedy, Jessica Bardwil, Caitlin Dodson, Albert Park.